Celebrate the Season

Let It
Snow!

Let It Snow!

by
Taylor Garland

Little, Brown and Company
New York Boston

Copyright © 2018 by Hachette Book Group

Cover/title page art © 2018 cynoclub/Shutterstock.com (cat and dog), Didecs/Shutterstock.com (ribbon), digieye/Shutterstock.com (bow/frame), olegganko/Shutterstock.com (snowflake background). Cover design by Cassie Gonzales. Cover copyright © 2018 by Hachette Book Group, Inc.

Hachette Book Group supports the right to free expression and the value of copyright. The purpose of copyright is to encourage writers and artists to produce the creative works that enrich our culture.

The scanning, uploading, and distribution of this book without permission is a theft of the author's intellectual property. If you would like permission to use material from the book (other than for review purposes), please contact permissions@hbgusa.com. Thank you for your support of the author's rights.

Little, Brown and Company
Hachette Book Group
1290 Avenue of the Americas, New York, NY 10104
Visit us at LBYR.com

First Edition: October 2018

Little, Brown and Company is a division of Hachette Book Group, Inc. The Little, Brown name and logo are trademarks of Hachette Book Group, Inc.

The publisher is not responsible for websites (or their content) that are not owned by the publisher.

Library of Congress Control Number: 2018940979

ISBNs: 978-0-316-41297-1 (pbk), 978-0-316-51891-8 (ebook)

Printed in the United States of America

LSC-C

Paperback: 10 9 8 7 6 5 4 3 2 1

Chapter 1

Chloe Warner wriggled under her bed, sneezing as dust tickled her nose. She hadn't used her suitcase since last summer—more than five months ago—and she definitely hadn't dealt with the army of dust bunnies that had sprung up since then, either. But she didn't care about that right now. In an hour, Chloe and her dad would be hitting the road for an incredible weekend at the Lodge Resort in the Pocono Mountains. And in three days, Christmas would be here!

Chloe had been counting down to the pre-Christmas getaway ever since Dad had told her about it back in October. She'd spent hours swiping through the lodge's website on her phone, imagining what it would be like to sleep in one of the rustic log cabins or ski down a snowy slope. She'd picked out the perfect dress (and the perfect accessories) for the big party on Christmas Eve Eve. The one part of the trip that Chloe wasn't able to prepare for was what it would be like to meet Dad's girlfriend, Jessica, and Jessica's daughter, Sandy, for the very first time.

Dad had told Chloe all about Jessica—that's how Chloe knew how important Jessica was to him—but it was still hard to imagine what she'd be like in person. And it was even harder to imagine what Sandy would be like, probably because Dad had never met Sandy, so there wasn't much he could tell her. Would they like the same music? Share the same hobbies? Become besties? Or would they have nothing in common at all?

Soon Chloe wouldn't have to wonder anymore.

Soon she would know!

Jeans, snow pants, shirts, sweaters—Chloe tossed them all into her suitcase. She was a little more careful with her special dress for the party. It was made of cranberry-colored lace, with a matching slip in exactly the same color. Chloe carefully folded it and placed it right on top.

Chloe glanced over at the bed, where her dog, a cuddly white terrier named Charlie, watched her with bright, curious eyes.

"What do you think, Charlie?" Chloe asked as she held up two different shoes. "Black velvet shoes or sparkly silver ones?"

"Woof!" Charlie barked.

"I agree," Chloe said with a giggle. "Sparkly silver all the way!"

She sat on the edge of her bed and checked the list on her phone. She'd packed just about everything—her clothes, her shoes, her accessories, her snow gear. Her toiletries bag was tucked into a side pocket. But Chloe still couldn't shake the feeling that she'd forgotten something.

"What is it, Charlie?" she asked, scratching her pup behind his ears. "What did I forget?"

Suddenly, a knowing smile crossed Chloe's face. "Of course," she whispered. Chloe leaned across the bed for a framed photo on her bedside table. She couldn't leave her mom behind.

Chloe nestled the photo in the lacy folds of her party dress. Her mother had died a long time ago—Chloe had only a few vivid memories of her; the rest had grown hazy over the years—but before she fell asleep every night she still liked to look at the beautiful photo of her mother.

Chloe zipped her suitcase closed and whistled to Charlie. "Come on, buddy!" she called.

Thunk-thunk-thunk-thunk. The suitcase thudded so loudly as Chloe dragged it down the stairs that Dad poked his head out of his room to see what was making all the noise. "Hey! I would've carried your suitcase downstairs!" he called out.

"No worries! I've got it!" Chloe replied. Once she reached the first floor, she wheeled the suitcase over to the front door, where she'd already left her backpack and a duffel bag packed with Charlie's food, leash, and dishes. She was happy Dad had managed to find a hotel that allowed Charlie to stay with them. The next few minutes passed by in a blur as Dad and Chloe loaded up the car. Then Chloe settled Charlie into his special dog bed in the back seat before she climbed in and fastened her seat belt. It was almost time to go!

"Ready?" Dad asked.

"Ready!" she replied.

"Then let's hit the road!" Dad announced as he started down the driveway. Chloe reached for her backpack to check the inside pocket one more time. She already knew that she'd packed Charlie's medicine—in fact, it was the very first thing she had packed—but she wanted to be certain before they were all the way in the mountains.

"Got everything?" Dad asked with a quick sideways glance at Chloe.

"Yes," she replied. "At least, I think so. And whatever I forgot, I'll just have to do without."

Dad chuckled. "We're spending the weekend at a three-star resort in the Poconos, not going on a mountaineering expedition," he told her. "There will be plenty of stores and shops if there's anything you need."

"Thanks, Dad—I know," Chloe said. "I just want everything to be perfect!"

Chloe inhaled deeply, breathing in the scent of the miniature pine tree that she and Dad had bought as a surprise for Jessica and Sandy. The sharp, piney smell filled the car and made it feel even more like Christmastime.

"Can't believe it's finally here," Dad said, breaking the silence. "Are you excited?"

"Are you kidding?" Chloe laughed. "I've been thinking about this trip nonstop! It's going to be incredible! Do you think Sandy and Jessica will get there before we do?"

"It depends on when they leave," Dad said. "Apparently, Sandy tends to sleep in. But Jessica said she'd do her best to get them on the road by ten o'clock."

"There's no way I could've slept late today," Chloe said. "I could barely sleep last night, either."

"Same here," Dad replied. "I'm so glad that you'll finally be able to meet Jessica. She's...she's really special."

Chloe glanced at Dad out of the corner of her eye, but he was focused on the road ahead. There was something about his voice that filled her with quivery excitement. It gave her the courage to ask the question that had been on her mind for months.

"Dad?" she began. "Are you going to ask Jessica to marry you?"

"Marry me?" Dad repeated. He started to laugh—a laugh that was both surprised and kind. "I don't know, Chloe. Marriage is a big commitment...one that should last a lifetime. We're not quite there yet. But Jessica means a lot to me, which is why I'm so excited for you two to meet. It's way past time for the most important ladies in my life to finally know each other."

"Got it," Chloe said. "I was just thinking...if you marry Jessica...then Sandy would be, like, my sister. *Stepsister*—whatever."

"That would be a big change, wouldn't it?" Dad asked.

"The sister I've always wanted!" Chloe joked. At least, she tried to make a joke. But in her heart, she'd always longed for a sibling. A sister—a sister her own age—would be like a dream come true.

Don't get carried away, Chloe told herself. After all, she'd never even met Sandy before.

But there was no harm in hoping—right?

❄ ❄ ❄

Two hours later, Dad and Chloe finally arrived at the lodge. The lobby had been so extensively decorated—there were swooping pine garlands, strands of twinkling lights, and enormous Christmas trees everywhere Chloe looked—that she didn't even mind the wait while Dad checked in.

"All set!" Dad finally announced. He handed Chloe her own key. "Keep this in a safe place, okay? We'll be staying in Sugar Plum Cottage."

"Sugar Plum Cottage?" Chloe repeated with a grin.

Dad grinned back. "They rename all the cottages for December," he explained. "Jessica and Sandy are in Mistletoe Cottage—which is just a short walk from ours."

Chloe's heart started to beat a little faster. "Do you mean—are they here?" she asked.

"They sure are. Jessica texted me twenty minutes

ago," Dad told her. "Let's get settled into our cottage and then we can—"

"Let's go over there right now!" Chloe said in excitement.

Dad chuckled. "All right, all right. But let's at least bring our luggage inside first," he said. "And maybe we should wait a little while to bring them the Christmas tree."

Chloe giggled. "It would probably look pretty weird if we just showed up with a tree without any warning," she replied.

Together, Dad and Chloe unloaded the car and took a quick tour of Sugar Plum Cottage. It was filled with rustic decorations—patchwork quilts, woven baskets, lamps in the shape of lanterns, and a weathered pine box filled with chopped-up wood by the fireplace.

"Hey, we have three bedrooms," Chloe said. "Does that mean Charlie gets his own room?"

"If he wants it," Dad said. "But I have a feeling he'll be sticking close to you, like always."

"Which room is mine?" she asked.

"Whichever one you want," Dad told her.

9

Chloe finally decided on the bedroom with a window seat that offered an amazing view of the snow-covered mountains. She didn't want to waste time unpacking, but there was one important thing Chloe wanted to do before she, Dad, and Charlie set off for Mistletoe Cottage. She unzipped her suitcase and pulled out Mom's photo. Once the photo was sitting on her bedside table, Chloe almost felt like she was at home. She adjusted the frame so that she could see Mom's loving smile better.

"Here goes," Chloe whispered to the photo. "Wish me luck!"

Chapter 2

On the walk over to Mistletoe Cottage, Chloe held on tightly to Charlie's leash. He was so excited by all the wild and unusual woodland smells that he was frolicking around like a puppy! It was almost impossible to keep him on the path.

"Char*lieeeee*," she groaned. "Stick with me, please. We're not wandering in the woods right now."

"It's hard to say who's more excited—you or Charlie," Dad teased Chloe.

But Chloe's attention was focused on something else: a carved wooden sign that read MISTLETOE

COTTAGE in bright red letters. "Dad! Look! There it is!" Chloe cried. "We're here!"

"I think I see Sandy looking out the window," Dad said.

Chloe caught a glimpse of her, too—but just as quickly, Sandy disappeared behind the curtain.

"Why don't you and Charlie go ahead and knock on the door," Dad told Chloe. "I'll be right behind you."

Chloe didn't need to be told twice. She and Charlie jogged the rest of the way to Mistletoe Cottage. On the doorstep, Chloe paused for a moment to catch her breath. Then she knocked three times.

The woman who opened the door had short chestnut-colored hair. She smiled brightly. "Chloe? Hi! I'm Jessica!" she said warmly. "Come on in."

"Hi," Chloe said, suddenly feeling a little shy. She'd tried to imagine this moment so many times—but now that it was here, she wasn't quite sure what to say.

A girl—who had to be Sandy—was standing a few feet behind Jessica. She looked just like her mom, except her hair was much longer and twisted into a loose braid on one side.

"Hey," Chloe said, stepping forward. "I'm—"

Then she saw it: a cat. A beautiful gray cat rubbing against Sandy's ankles.

Unfortunately, Charlie saw it at the same time. He lunged forward a split second before Chloe could tighten her grip on his leash. The leash slipped through her grasp—

"Charlie! No!" Chloe exclaimed. But it was too late. He was already barking wildly as he charged at Sandy's cat.

"Stop! Stop! *Stop!*" Sandy screamed, her voice more high-pitched with every word. "Make him stop! He's going to kill Elsa!"

No, he's not! Chloe wanted to yell back—but she knew that if Charlie heard her speak loudly, he'd only get more riled up. She knelt down and used her softest, most soothing voice. "Come here, boy, come here," she cooed.

But Charlie was having way too much fun to stop now. He was running in fast, wild circles, barking his head off at Elsa, who was yowling and hissing with fear as she tried to escape. The cat was obviously miserable—her back was arched, her fur standing on end—but Charlie was just a dog. He didn't understand.

"Why isn't anyone doing anything?" Sandy cried. "Please! Don't let him hurt Elsa!"

Dad arrived just in time. "Charlie!" he said sternly. "Come *here*!"

Jessica hurried to the kitchen and returned with a container of kitty treats. "Want a treat, Charlie?" she said in a singsong voice, shaking the container.

"No!" Chloe said—and this time her voice *was* loud. "He can't have—"

Crash!

At that moment, Elsa ducked under the side table—and even though Charlie was a small dog, he was too big to follow her without knocking into one of the table legs. As the table shuddered, a lamp on top of it began to wobble....

"Whoa!" Dad said, lunging forward to grab the lamp before it fell.

"Don't grab the lamp—grab the dog!" Sandy shrieked.

"Hey!" Chloe began. But then she caught a glimpse of Sandy's face, all blotchy and red; her eyes were filled with tears. *Sandy's really terrified*, Chloe realized.

From under the table, Elsa's hisses turned into an angry spitting sound. She growled, a low, guttural sound that was audible even over Charlie's happy barks. Chloe came up with a plan. She'd shimmy under the table, grab Charlie, and take him outside so Elsa—and Sandy—could have a few minutes to calm down.

Chloe dropped to the floor just in time to see Elsa's gray paw slash through the air. Charlie yipped, a terrible, heartbreaking noise, and whimpered as he backed out from under the table—right into Chloe's arms. A thin red line of blood from Elsa's scratch welled up on his nose.

"Dad?" Chloe said. "Charlie's bleeding!"

Dad crossed the room and took a good look at Charlie's nose. "He'll be okay," Dad assured Chloe. "I'm sure his pride is wounded worse than his nose."

"Oh, Elsa!" Jessica groaned, sounding embarrassed. "I'm so sorry. We cut her nails yesterday and everything."

"It wasn't Elsa's fault!" Sandy protested. She was

crouched next to the table, shaking the kitty treats in hopes of luring Elsa out. "She was just trying to defend herself from that vicious, crazy dog!"

"Charlie is *not* vicious!" Chloe exclaimed. "I mean, maybe he gets a little crazy sometimes, like when he sees a squirrel or a blue jay or—"

"Or my cat," Sandy muttered.

"I know you don't know Charlie at all, but you have to trust me," Chloe insisted. "He would *never* hurt Elsa. He just wanted to play with her. I promise."

Sandy didn't say anything, but from the look on her face, Chloe could tell she didn't believe her.

"Let's start over," Chloe continued, hoping to lighten the mood. "I see you've met my dog, Charlie. And I'm Chloe."

"I already know who you are," Sandy replied.

"Sandy!" Jessica said with a frown.

"What?" Sandy asked. "Isn't the whole introduction thing kind of pointless? We all know who we are. It's not a huge crowd."

Suddenly, Chloe's dad sneezed—an enormous, shoulder-shuddering sneeze that was so loud everyone turned to look at him.

"Sor—" Dad started to say, but another massive sneeze cut him off.

For the briefest moment, Chloe thought he was trying to be funny. Then she remembered.

"Dad!" Chloe exclaimed as her eyes darted over to Sandy, who was still snuggling Elsa. "Your allergies!" It had been so long since her dad had been around cats that Chloe had forgotten how allergic he was.

"Allergies?" Jessica asked.

"Did I forget to mention I'm allergic to cats?" Dad asked with a sheepish smile.

"Did I forget to mention that we have one?" Jessica asked, smiling back. There was something about their smiles—Chloe couldn't quite put her finger on it, but it was almost like they were sharing more than a smile. It was like they were sharing a secret.

"Seriously, Mom?" Sandy asked. "How could you *forget* to tell him about Elsa? She's part of the family!"

"Sorry, sweet pea," Jessica replied. "It just slipped my mind."

Ah-choo! Dad sneezed again. A look of concern flickered across Jessica's face.

"Sandy," she began.

It was like Sandy knew what Jessica was going to say next. She wrapped her arms even tighter around Elsa and shook her head.

"You'll have to keep Elsa in your room while Tom is here," Jessica said. Her voice was even—she didn't sound mad or anything—but there was a no-arguing tone in it that was obvious to everyone.

Sandy didn't move a muscle, and she didn't say a word. The only sound was when Dad sneezed *again*.

A silent look passed between Jessica and Sandy for a long moment that was uncomfortable for everyone. Then, with a loud sigh, Sandy spun around and marched out of the room.

The next sound was the loud *slam* of a door.

Jessica shook her head. "Please excuse me," she said before disappearing after Sandy.

Chloe hadn't done anything wrong, but she still felt terrible. This was *not* how she had pictured her first meeting with Sandy and Jessica.

If only Dad wasn't allergic—

If only Charlie hadn't chased Elsa—

If only there was something Chloe could do to fix everything—

That's when she had a great idea.

"Dad!" she said in an excited whisper. "Let's go get the tree!"

"Now?" he asked, sounding uncertain. "Maybe we should wait until—"

Chloe shook her head. "No, when they get back, it will be really awkward," she replied. "Jessica and Sandy are probably, like, fighting right now. But if we surprise them with the tree..."

"I see where you're going with this," Dad said. "I think the tree will be just what we need to bring back the Christmas spirit."

"Great! Let's go get it," Chloe said.

A few minutes later, they returned with the table-top tree. The scent immediately filled the room, making the cottage feel much more Christmassy.

"The little tree was a great idea, Chloe," Dad told her. "They're going to be so surprised."

"I hope so," Chloe replied. "Quick! Let's see if we can get the lights on before Jessica and Sandy come back!"

The tree was small enough that Chloe and Dad were able to wrap the strand of lights around it in no time. Dad held the plug out to Chloe. "Would you like to do the honors?" he asked.

Chloe reached for the cord—but stopped herself just before she plugged it into the wall. "You know what? I think I'll ask Sandy if she wants to plug in the tree," she said.

Before Dad could respond, Chloe heard footsteps coming down the hall. Her heart sped up a little bit as Sandy and Jessica returned to the living room. More than anything, Chloe hoped that the little tree would be a fresh start, a way to help them get the trip back on track.

"What's this?" Jessica asked.

"Surprise! It's a little Christmas tree!" Chloe exclaimed. She immediately wished she'd said something—*anything*—else. *Duh, of course it's a little tree*, Chloe thought. *Way to state the obvious.*

But she pushed on, hoping that she wouldn't keep sounding so, well, desperate. And dumb.

"It doesn't feel like Christmas without a tree," Chloe continued. "So we—we thought we'd surprise you. Here—do you want to plug it in?"

Sandy stared at the cord in Chloe's outstretched hand like she didn't know what it was.

"We already have a tree," Sandy finally said. "Back home. We already decorated it, too."

Chloe dropped her hand, feeling even more embarrassed. *Maybe Sandy is upset because this tree doesn't even have any ornaments*, she thought.

"I *love* this little tree!" Jessica said in happy voice that was maybe just a little too loud. "What a great surprise, Chloe and Tom! It's just what our cottage needed. I can't wait to decorate it!"

"We, um, we didn't bring any ornaments, actually," Chloe spoke up. "But I have a ton of stuff to *make* ornaments! It's all here in this bag—sparkly paper and foil and ribbon and—"

"*Mom*," Sandy said, staring straight at Jessica. Now Chloe was even more confused. Had she said something that upset Sandy? Or was Sandy still mad about Charlie and Elsa's fight? Or the fact that Elsa had to stay in Sandy's bedroom?

Chloe glanced uncertainly at her dad. He looked as confused as she felt. "Maybe the tree wasn't such a great idea," she said. "We can take it back to our cottage."

"No!" Jessica insisted. "I love it. It was so thoughtful—the perfect surprise! And I'd love to make some ornaments with you, Chloe. Let's see what you brought."

With a shy, sideways glance at Sandy, Chloe brought over the bag of her best crafting supplies.

"Ooh, I love this glitter paper!" Jessica exclaimed. "The gold piece will be perfect for the star on top."

"Check out this foil, too," Chloe said, feeling heartened. "So easy—all we have to do is cut out circles and they'll look like shiny Christmas orbs. Of course, my circles look more like squiggly ovals. I'm not so great at drawing—"

"You could use this."

When Sandy spoke, everyone turned to her. She brought over the canister of kitty treats, which had a perfectly round lid.

"Yes!" Chloe exclaimed. "Just trace it and cut it out, right?"

Sandy nodded. "I think that will work."

Sandy sat down in the chair across from Chloe

and reached for a package of coffee filters. She held it up and made a funny face. "Is your tree hooked on caffeine?" she cracked.

"Not exactly," Chloe said, smiling back. "I thought we could cut those into snowflakes."

"Cool," Sandy replied, reaching for the scissors.

"Who wants some hot cocoa?" Jessica suddenly asked. "We've got mini marshmallows *and* whipped cream!"

"Yum! I do," Chloe said.

"Me too," added Sandy.

"Tom, would you help me in the kitchen?" Jessica asked.

"The kitchen? Sure. Of course," Dad said quickly.

As soon as they were out of the room, Sandy laughed under her breath. "Way to be obvious, *Mom*," she said. Chloe laughed, too. Dad and Jessica hadn't been very subtle.

"Bet you anything they're talking about us right now," Sandy added.

"Yeah. You're probably right," Chloe said. "I think they talk about us a lot, actually. After my dad sees your mom, he's always like, 'Sandy scored a three-pointer' and 'Sandy got a ribbon in the science fair.'"

Sandy stared intently at the coffee filter she was cutting. "My mom never tells me anything," she said.

Whoops, Chloe thought. Just when things were getting better, she'd blown it—again. "My dad doesn't tell me that much, honestly," she said. "Just, like, your basketball games, mainly. I play, too."

Sandy looked up, her eyes bright with curiosity. "Oh, yeah? Which position?"

"Guard," Chloe replied.

"Cool. I'm a guard, too," Sandy said.

Chloe already knew that, but she wasn't going to tell Sandy. "Awesome," she replied. "Are you on any other teams?"

"Nope. Basketball's my favorite," Sandy said.

There was an awkward pause. Chloe tried to think of another topic.

"I like to cook—do you?" she asked.

"Not really—that's more my mom's thing," Sandy replied. "But…I like to watch people cooking."

"Really?" Chloe replied. "Like, cooking shows?"

Sandy nodded. "I could watch them for *hours*,"

she said. "Actually, I have watched them for hours! Last weekend, one of the food channels had a Christmas-cookie marathon—"

"I saw that!" Chloe exclaimed.

"I watched it for, like, six hours!" Sandy told her.

"Me too!" Chloe said. "Then I was inspired to make florentines—you know, those lacy ones with the chocolate in the middle—"

"I remember! They looked so good. Were they delicious?"

"Well…" Chloe began. "They *looked* delicious, but I accidentally used baking chocolate instead of semisweet chocolate for the chocolate layer. They were so bitter, we couldn't even eat them! I threw the whole batch away!"

"No! That's tragic!" Sandy cried, cracking up. "I thought you liked to cook!"

"I do like to cook!" Chloe replied. "I never said I was any *good* at it!"

"Oh, no—look what I did," Sandy said, holding up her coffee-filter snowflake. She'd laughed so hard that she had accidentally cut it in half—which made both girls laugh even harder.

Suddenly, Chloe stopped laughing. "Where's Charlie?" she asked, glancing around the room. "Usually if I'm sitting down, he's got his head on my feet."

"Don't worry," Sandy told her. "He's right here. He's got his head on *my* feet."

Chloe was so surprised she ducked under the table to see for herself. "Charlie! Don't bother Sandy," she scolded him. "Come here, boy."

"It's okay," Sandy said quickly. "I don't mind. He's like my own personal foot warmer."

"Okay...if you're sure he's not bothering you..." Chloe said as she returned to her seat.

"Nah, he's a good boy," Sandy said. "How old is he?"

"Nine," Chloe said. "We got him after..."

"After what?" Sandy asked when Chloe's voice trailed off.

"Oh. Sorry. I spaced out a little. After my...third birthday. Charlie was a Christmas present, actually," Chloe said, quickly covering. Inside, though, she was yelling at herself to be more careful. She'd almost said *after my mom died*. Thankfully, though, Chloe had caught herself just in time. She knew from experience that there was no quicker way to derail a conversation than to mention her mom. Nobody ever knew what to say when they found out that her mom had died.

If Chloe was acting weird, Sandy didn't seem to notice. "Nine? I can't believe it! He still acts like a puppy!" she said.

"Actually, he has some health problems," Chloe told her. "He got really sick last year and now he has to be on a special diet and take medicine every day."

"Aww, poor Charlie," Sandy said, reaching down to scratch his ears. "That must have been so scary."

"It was awful," Chloe agreed.

"I've been there with Elsa—but in her case, it was entirely her own fault," Sandy replied.

"What do you mean?" asked Chloe.

"She likes to eat things she shouldn't," Sandy explained. "Ribbon or tinsel or string—stuff like that. That's why..."

Sandy's voice trailed off as she gestured at the small pile of ribbon she'd made on the table.

"Oh!" Chloe exclaimed. "Is that why you didn't want to decorate the tree?"

Sandy nodded. "At least, not with ribbons," she said. "One time when Elsa ate ribbon, it made her really sick. She almost needed surgery."

"Yikes," Chloe said, making a sympathetic face. "That's terrible." She impulsively reached forward and grabbed the ribbons, then shoved them in her backpack. "I'll keep these zipped up until I can stash them at our cottage," she promised. "We have plenty of other stuff for decorating the tree."

Sandy flashed Chloe a grateful smile. "Thank you," she said. "I love Elsa so much. If she got sick like that again..."

"I know *exactly* what you mean," Chloe replied. She smiled at Sandy as her heart filled up with hope. The trip may have gotten off to a rocky start...but Chloe had a feeling it was only going to get better from here!

Chapter 3

After the girls finished decorating the tree, Sandy turned to Chloe. "I was thinking," she began. "You and Elsa didn't really get to meet each other properly; everything was so...crazy. Do you want to come see her?"

"Definitely!" Chloe replied with a big smile. She didn't want to jinx things, but Chloe couldn't help thinking that she and Sandy were on the way to becoming friends. Maybe even best friends!

Chloe followed Sandy to her room. "Be ready," Sandy said over her shoulder as she opened the door just a crack. "Elsa does *not* like being trapped. She'll probably try to bolt."

"I'm ready," Chloe assured her.

In one fast motion, Sandy opened the door and knelt down to preemptively block Elsa from escaping. "Go, go, go, go!" she urged Chloe, who dissolved into giggles as she scrambled through the doorway. Sandy was right behind her, and both girls cracked up as they crashed onto the braided rug in the middle of the room.

Elsa, who was snuggled on a pillow on one of the twin beds the whole time, opened her eyes. She didn't look impressed.

"She's so pretty," Chloe said. "Do you think she'd let me pet her?"

"Sure," Sandy said. She reached over and pulled Elsa into her lap. "She's actually very cuddly when she's not being chased by a dog she's never met before."

Chloe's smile faded.

"I'm joking!" Sandy quickly said. "Charlie's a great dog. He just...got a little carried away. Here—do you want to hold her?"

"Yes!" Chloe exclaimed. She settled on the floor

and held out her arms. Sandy carefully passed Elsa to Chloe.

"Oh! She's purring!" Chloe said quietly so that she wouldn't startle Elsa.

"She likes you," Sandy said.

"You think so?" Chloe asked, resting her ear against Elsa's fur. "Because I *love* her. I always wanted a cat, but... you know. My dad's allergies."

"That's too bad," Sandy said sympathetically.

"If he would get allergy shots, it would help a lot," Chloe confided. "But my dad didn't see the point, especially because I love dogs, too." Then a knowing smile crossed her face. "Of course, he might be more *interested* in getting those shots now."

Sandy reached over and pulled Elsa back into her lap. "Oh?" she said.

"Of course! My dad would do anything for your mom," Chloe said. "He's totally crazy about her! It would be, like, embarrassing if it wasn't so sweet."

Sandy didn't answer.

"Trust me, he's not about to let some little cat allergy get in the way," Chloe said.

At last, Sandy spoke. "Get in the way of what?"

"Their relationship!" Chloe said. "They seem really happy together, huh? I mean, *really* happy. I wouldn't be surprised if my dad asks your mom to marry him! Wouldn't it—"

"Let me stop you right there," Sandy interrupted. Her voice was colder than the icicles hanging from the eaves outside. "I have literally no idea what you're talking about."

Chloe blinked in confusion. "I—our parents—"

"No." Sandy shut her down. "Absolutely not. I'm sorry to be the one to tell you this, but my parents are probably getting back together."

"But—"

"And even if they weren't, my mom would *never* marry your dad," Sandy continued, talking right over Chloe. "He is *definitely* not her type."

Chloe's knuckles dug into the rug as she pushed herself off the floor. She walked to the door with perfect posture and steady steps, aware of every muscle in her body as she tried to will away the tears that stung her eyes. She wasn't going to cry in front of Sandy. She wasn't going to give her the satisfaction.

Because that was what Sandy wanted, right?

32

Chloe couldn't think of any other reason why she would be so, well, *mean*. She didn't understand it. One minute, Sandy seemed sweet and fun and cool. The next minute, she was insulting Chloe's dad, acting like he wasn't good enough for her mom. Acting like her mom wouldn't ever lower herself to date him—let alone get married.

Chloe paused in the hallway. *Does Sandy know something I don't know?* she wondered. What if Jessica had told Sandy that she and Dad were just friends? What if—what if she'd told Sandy that she was going to break up with Dad? For a moment, Chloe felt sick. What if Dad *was* planning to propose someday—but Jessica was already planning to dump him?

It was too horrible to think about.

Chloe was sure of one thing, though. She wanted to leave Mistletoe Cottage and never look back. *Dad and I can have our own fun weekend*, she thought fiercely as she strode toward the living room. *Who needs them?*

"Dad, I want—" Chloe announced as she burst into the living room.

Then she stopped short.

There were Dad and Jessica, slow dancing in the light of the little Christmas tree. From where she was standing, Chloe could see Jessica better than Dad. Jessica's head rested against his shoulder, her eyes were closed, and there was the happiest smile on her face. Even from across the room, Chloe could tell that there was nowhere Jessica would rather be.

So what was Sandy talking about?

Dad and Jessica stopped dancing, and Chloe wished she hadn't interrupted them.

"Hey there, sweetie," Dad said, a look of concern on his face. "What's wrong?"

"Nothing's wrong," Chloe said, forcing herself to smile even as her face turned red. She'd never been good at lying. "I'm just—tired."

"Tired?" Dad repeated as he crossed the room. "I hope you're not coming down with something. Your face is flushed. Do you feel feverish?"

Chloe ducked away from Dad's hand as he reached for her forehead. "No, I'm fine. Just tired," she said. "I was so excited about the trip that I barely slept last night—remember?"

That part, at least, was true.

"Would it be okay if I go back to our cabin and rest for a while?" Chloe asked.

Jessica and Dad exchanged a glance. They always seemed to be talking without any words.

"I'm pretty tired, too," Jessica said. "I was up late finishing a project for work so I could take a few days off. I'll probably need to lie down for a while this afternoon... unless you want me falling asleep at the dinner table!"

Chloe smiled again. She could tell that Jessica was trying really hard to connect with her... and to lighten the mood.

"Nothing wrong with a little afternoon siesta," Dad announced. "Let's plan to meet at the restaurant at six o'clock for dinner. I'll call and make a reservation."

"Thanks, Tom," Jessica said. She looked like she wanted to say something else.

Oh, please don't make Sandy come out here to say goodbye to me, Chloe worried.

Luckily, though, all Jessica said was, "Hope you get some good rest, Chloe."

"And you, too," Dad said to Jessica. "The restaurant up at the lodge is supposed to be excellent—definitely not a meal you want to sleep through."

"Come here, Charlie," Chloe said with her special whistle. He trotted over so that she could clip his leash to his collar. Then Chloe, Charlie, and Dad walked outside.

The pebbles on the path crunched under their feet as they set off for their cabin. When they were out of earshot, Dad sighed with relief. "Phew! I'm glad that's over with," he said.

"What do you mean?" Chloe asked, surprised. Dad was crazy about Jessica—right? Why would he be glad to leave?

"All the pressure," Dad explained. "It's stressful to meet people for the first time! I was pretty nervous this morning."

"You were?" Chloe asked. "I had no idea."

"Oh, sure," Dad told her. "What if you didn't like Jessica? What if you and Sandy didn't get along? What if Sandy didn't like me? Well—actually—I don't think Sandy *does* like me—"

Chloe's face turned red again. "That's her problem,

not yours," she said, surprised by the anger in her voice. "You're an awesome dad!"

"Yes, I know," Dad said in that funny voice that always made Chloe laugh. "But this kind of thing is hard for everyone. A lot of stress. A lot of pressure. And—just between you and me—Sandy's still struggling with her parents' divorce."

"I don't get it," Chloe replied. "I thought her parents got divorced, like, three years ago."

"They *separated* three years ago," Dad corrected her. "The actual divorce just became final last September."

"Oh," Chloe said. She still didn't understand why Sandy would be having a hard time. After all, she'd had three years to get used to it.

"Anyway. Just something to keep in mind," Dad said. He rubbed his eyes as they approached their cabin.

"Your allergies?" Chloe guessed.

Dad nodded. "They'll probably get better now that we're in a cat-free zone," he joked. "Don't worry about me, sweetie. Just get some rest."

"Thanks, Dad," Chloe said as she gave him a hug.

✳ ✳ ✳

A couple of hours later, Chloe's eyes opened. She sat up on the bed, momentarily confused, until she remembered that she was in a cabin at the lodge. Chloe stood up, stretched, and wandered into the living room. "Dad?" she called out. "Charlie?"

There was no sound—not even the clinking of Charlie's tags.

That's when Chloe noticed a note on the table.

Hey, sleeping beauty—I went to the lodge in search of some allergy medicine. Charlie has accompanied me. Back soon. Love, Dad

Chloe had just finished reading Dad's note when she heard a key turning in the lock.

"Look who's up," Dad said, grinning at Chloe.

"Successful shopping trip?" Chloe asked as she glanced at the large paper bag in his hand.

"I bought every kind of allergy medicine they sell," Dad said. "And one of these, too. Think fast!"

Chloe's hand flew up just in time to catch the chocolate bar Dad tossed to her.

"Attagirl," he said. "Great reflexes! But don't ruin your appetite for dinner. We're going to meet Jessica and Sandy soon."

"I'll just have a bite or two," Chloe replied as she tore open the wrapper. It was her favorite kind.

Then Dad's face grew serious. "Chloe," he began, "I don't want you to worry, but Charlie got sick on our walk."

Chloe swallowed hard. Suddenly, she didn't feel like eating the candy bar. She didn't feel like eating anything. "His gastritis?" she asked. Her voice sounded higher than usual.

Dad nodded. "I was wondering—is there any chance you forgot to give him his medicine this morning?"

"No way!" Chloe exclaimed. "I *always* give it to him!"

She leaned over to pick up Charlie and buried her face in his fur.

"I know you do," Dad said, patting Chloe's back. "I just thought, maybe with all the excitement of packing and getting ready for the trip…"

Chloe paused, racking her brain as she thought back to that morning. *Had* she given Charlie his medicine? Or had she been in such a rush to pack everything that she could have forgotten?

Chloe shook her head. "I definitely gave it to him," she told Dad. "I'm certain. It's the first thing I do every morning. Even before I eat breakfast."

"Okay," Dad said. "That's what I figured."

"But if Charlie took his medicine, why is he sick?" Chloe asked anxiously. "He hasn't eaten anything weird. He hasn't had a flare-up in ages. Oh, Dad, do you think—"

"Nope," Dad said firmly, cutting Chloe off before she could even say the words. "I don't think there's any reason to panic. Remember, it's been an exciting—and stressful—day for Charlie, too. New people, new places, a long car ride…"

"Don't forget an angry cat," Chloe said, remembering Elsa's claws swiping across Charlie's nose.

"A *very* angry cat," Dad agreed. "I'm not a vet, but

I'd guess that would be enough to upset his stomach. Remember what Dr. Garcia said to do when Charlie has a gastritis attack?"

Chloe nodded. "Watch him carefully for twenty-four hours," she said. "Make sure he has lots of water, takes his medicine, and only eats his special food."

"And that's exactly what we're going to do," Dad promised. "And if Charlie doesn't get better—or if he gets worse—we'll call Dr. Garcia right away. I promise."

"Thanks, Dad," Chloe said. As she stroked Charlie's fur, he stretched and yawned, making Chloe and her dad laugh. Charlie didn't seem sick, but Chloe still couldn't help worrying about him. She couldn't bear the thought of Charlie getting really ill and going back to the animal hospital again.

Dad stood up. "I'm going to figure out what to wear tonight," he told Chloe. "The restaurant looks a little fancier than I expected. I don't want to get kicked out for not wearing a tie."

"I forgot we were going out to eat," Chloe said. "Can I stay here with Charlie?"

"Let's see how he does for the rest of the afternoon,"

Dad told her. "If Charlie gets worse, of course we'll cancel our dinner reservation. But if he's doing okay, we should both go. This is a great chance for you to get to know Jessica and Sandy a little better."

"Okay," Chloe sighed. She'd much rather stay with Charlie than eat dinner with Sandy. But if Charlie had to get even sicker for Chloe to stay in, dinner with Sandy sounded great.

Chapter 2

By the time Chloe and Dad had to leave for dinner, Charlie seemed like he was feeling better. Chloe could tell by the way he waited by his food dish, wagging his tail expectantly. "Just a little bit, Charlie," she told him as she measured a few spoonfuls of his special food into the bowl. "Then you can have a little more at bedtime with your medicine."

A few minutes later, Chloe and Dad set off toward the lodge. Small diamond-shaped lights illuminated the path, gleaming in the darkness. Up on the hill, the lodge glowed with light, and Chloe could imagine how cozy and warm it would be inside.

Chloe realized two things at the same time: It was really, really cold, and she was really, really hungry. She started walking faster.

When they arrived at the restaurant, Chloe decided to thaw by the roaring fire in the lobby while Dad checked in with the maître d'. She glanced around the lobby, but there was no sign of Jessica or Sandy. *Maybe Sandy didn't want to come to dinner, either*, Chloe thought.

Just then, she felt a tap on her shoulder. Chloe was surprised when she saw Jessica—and not Dad—standing behind her. "I thought that was you," Jessica said with a warm smile.

"Hi, Jessica," Chloe replied. She glanced around but didn't see Sandy anywhere. *Maybe she really did stay at their cottage*, Chloe thought.

"Sandy and I got here a little early, so we've already been seated," Jessica said, almost as if she could read Chloe's thoughts. "Come with me. The menu is amazing—it's going to be hard to decide what to order."

"Dad—" Chloe began.

"I already pointed him in the right direction,"

Jessica assured her. "But we'd better hurry before he and Sandy eat all the bread!"

Jessica kept talking as she led Chloe through the dining room. "How was your afternoon? Did you get some rest?" she asked.

"A little," Chloe replied. "How about you?"

"Yes, thankfully," Jessica replied. "I'm happy to report that there's no risk of my falling asleep in my entree tonight."

"Well, *that's* good," Chloe replied. "But what about dessert?"

Jessica held up her hands. "I can't make any promises," she replied. Then she and Chloe started laughing at the same time.

Jessica's pretty cool, Chloe thought. *And funny, too. I can see why Dad likes her so much.*

They were still laughing when they arrived at their table, which was tucked in a corner between another fireplace and an enormous picture window overlooking the mountainside. Chloe sat in a chair across from Sandy, who seemed really interested in her napkin all of a sudden.

"Hi," Chloe said.

"Hey," Sandy replied, not looking up.

"So what did you do this afternoon?" Chloe asked Sandy.

Sandy shrugged. "Nothing. Hung out."

There was nowhere to go from there. Chloe couldn't even think of a follow-up question. She gazed out the window at the dark winter sky, where far-off stars twinkled in the frosty night, and tried not to sigh. *I guess we're picking up right where we left off,* she thought.

"I was just telling Sandy about my shopping spree," Dad said, trying to lighten the mood. "Every allergy medicine in the gift shop! I could set up my very own pharmacy now. Specializing in allergy relief, of course."

"You probably won't need it, though," Sandy said. She was still staring at the table. "It's not like Elsa can even come out of my room when you're around. You'll probably never see her again."

Chloe snuck a glance at Jessica, who did *not* look pleased. But she simply took a deep breath and turned to Chloe. "Speaking of our sparring pets, how's Charlie's nose?" she asked.

"His nose?" Chloe repeated, momentarily forgetting about the scratch Elsa had given him. "Oh! Right! It seems fine. It's not bothering him at all. I'm more worried about..." Chloe's voice trailed off. It didn't seem appropriate to talk about Charlie's upset stomach at the dinner table.

"What's wrong?" Jessica asked.

"Charlie's got some chronic health problems," Dad explained. "Usually they're pretty much under control, but he was showing some symptoms this afternoon."

"Oh no!"

Everyone turned to look at Sandy. To Chloe's surprise, she looked genuinely concerned—like she really cared about what happened to Charlie. "Is that what you were telling me about this afternoon?" Sandy asked Chloe.

Chloe nodded. "I just don't know what made him sick," she explained. "He's been taking his medicine and eating his special diet—just like at home. Nothing is different."

"He was only sick once," Dad added. "I bet it had to do with all the stress and excitement of the trip.

Besides his walks around our neighborhood, old Charlie doesn't get out much."

"I hope it wasn't Elsa's fault," Sandy said, sounding worried. "Poor Charlie. I bet it was really stressful to get attacked by a cat."

"Well, Charlie wasn't exactly blameless," Dad said with a chuckle. "Hopefully he's learned his lesson...and some better manners, too. Anyway, he seemed fine by the time we left for dinner. I'm not worried."

I wish I could say the same, Chloe thought.

The waiter was hovering nearby, so everyone paused to examine the menu. After they placed their orders, Jessica pulled some brochures out of her purse.

"Sandy and I picked these up in the lobby," she explained as she passed them around the table. Chloe took one, even though she'd spent so much time on the resort website that she could have recited all the activities by heart.

"There's so much to do here!" Jessica continued. "I wish we could stay for a whole week. One weekend won't be long enough to even scratch the surface."

48

"So we'll just have to pack the most fun into tomorrow that we can," Dad said.

"Before the big party," Chloe added. She didn't want to miss the fancy Christmas party that the lodge threw every year. The pictures online were amazing.

"Yeah!" Sandy spoke up. "I got a new dress and everything."

"Me too!" Chloe exclaimed. "What does yours look like? Mine is cranberry and it has long sleeves."

"Mine is long-sleeved, too, but it's emerald green," Sandy told her.

"I bet that looks amazing with your eyes," Chloe said.

Sandy flashed her a smile, obviously pleased by the compliment. "Thanks! That's why I picked that color," she replied.

"Okay, party girls," Dad said in his teasing voice. "Our plans for tomorrow evening are clearly set in stone. But what about the rest of the day? Any thoughts?"

"I really, really, really want to go snow tubing," Sandy said right away. "I've never been before, but

I saw some videos online and it looks like so much fun."

"Yeah! I've never been snow tubing, either," Chloe said. "And I'd love to try skiing, too."

"I read some reviews about the winter sports here," Jessica spoke up. "Apparently, the lines for snow tubing are *really* long. If we go snow tubing, we might not have time for anything else, like shopping or skiing."

There was a pause before anyone spoke. Then Dad turned to Chloe. "I know you were really looking forward to skiing," he said. "But would you mind saving that for another trip? Maybe next winter?"

"I—" Chloe began. But Jessica was already talking.

"Actually, I'd love to go skiing, too," she said. "Maybe we could hit the slopes in the morning—and the shops in the afternoon! What do you think?"

Chloe grinned. That sounded like a great plan to her. But just as she was about to respond, she noticed Sandy's face. At first glance, it appeared frozen, like Sandy didn't want to show anyone how she was feeling. But there was so much pain in her eyes as she stared at Jessica that even Chloe could see it across the table.

"You know, let's all go snow tubing instead," Chloe said, making a split-second decision. "We can go shopping anytime. And skiing's not *that* important to me. I mostly want to do something outside, in the snow. If the lines for snow tubing are so long, it must be really incredible."

Dad reached over and gave Chloe's hand a quick squeeze. "You sure?" he asked in a low voice.

"Definitely," Chloe replied, smiling so big her cheeks hurt. "Snow tubing is going to be awesome!"

She looked over at Sandy again, hoping that they could get back on track.

But Sandy, still staring at Jessica, didn't seem to notice that Chloe was trying to catch her eye.

And she didn't say a word.

❄ ❄ ❄

No matter what anyone did, Sandy was practically silent for the rest of the meal. It was exhausting trying to carry on a conversation when one person refused to participate—and the harder everyone tried, the more sullen and silent Sandy stayed. Chloe couldn't wait for dinner to end.

"Can I interest anyone in dessert?" the waiter asked as he cleared their plates. "In addition to our dessert menu, the special tonight is hot-chocolate cake topped with peppermint ice cream."

"Hot chocolate in cake form?" Dad said, smiling at Chloe. "I know somebody who will want to try that!"

Ordinarily, Dad would've been right. But tonight, Chloe didn't want to stay at dinner one minute longer than she had to ... and not just because Sandy was acting so unfriendly.

"Actually, Dad, could we skip dessert tonight?" Chloe spoke up. "I want to get back to the cottage and make sure Charlie's still feeling better."

"That's the best reason for skipping dessert that I ever heard," Dad said, standing up. "Excuse us, ladies. We need to check on our furry patient."

"We'll walk back with you," Jessica said, signaling the waiter for the check.

"But, Mom—can't we stay for dessert?" Sandy

asked. It was the first time she'd spoken a full sentence in almost an hour.

Annoyance flickered across Jessica's face. "I—"

"Of course you should!" Dad said. "No reason why we all need to miss out."

Once again, Dad and Jessica exchanged a look. Chloe had a feeling they'd be texting later.

"Okay," Jessica finally said. "See you at breakfast tomorrow."

"I hope Charlie is okay," Sandy spoke up, surprising everyone again.

"Thanks," Chloe said stiffly. It wasn't easy to keep up with Sandy's moods.

Chloe was unusually quiet on the walk back to the cabin. It wasn't just her worry about Charlie that was weighing so heavily on her. Now Chloe was dreading having to spend the entire day with Sandy tomorrow.

Luckily, Charlie was waiting for them at the front door. From the way his tail was wagging, Chloe could tell that Charlie felt just fine—and was ready for his nighttime stroll *and* a little more food.

"Good boy!" Chloe said approvingly as Charlie

took big bites of his second small dinner. "Check it out, Dad! Charlie's appetite is back!"

"And his energy, too," Dad said with a laugh. He held up Charlie's leash. "Who wants to go for a walk?"

"Here, I can take him," Chloe offered, holding out her hand. "We'll just take a walk around the cottage."

"No, you stay inside where it's warm," Dad told her. "Charlie and I will be back in a few minutes."

After Dad took Charlie out, the cottage seemed bigger and quieter than usual. Chloe wandered into the kitchen and filled the teakettle with water. Sharing a cup of tea with Dad every night was one of Chloe's favorite bedtime rituals, so she'd made sure to pack their favorite kinds of tea.

The door opened then, and Dad and Charlie hurried inside out of the cold. "Good news," Dad announced. "Charlie did great on our walk. He didn't get sick at all!"

"That's not good news—it's *great* news," Chloe replied with a smile. "I made tea."

"I was hoping you would," Dad said, rubbing his

hands together. "It's colder than it looks outside. I bet the temperature is in the single digits."

When the tea was ready, Chloe and Dad carried the steaming mugs into the living room. Chloe curled up on the corner of the couch and stared into her cup. She didn't want to burden Dad with her worries about Sandy—but she was having trouble thinking about anything else.

"I can't believe the first day of our trip is over already," Dad began.

"Mm-hmm," Chloe said. She sipped her tea.

"Are you having fun?" asked Dad.

Chloe looked over at him and half smiled, half shrugged.

"That's what I thought," Dad replied. "You want to talk about it?"

"I guess," Chloe said, though she wasn't sure how to begin.

"Not quite what you expected?" Dad guessed.

"Yeah," Chloe said. "Jessica's great, though. Really great. I like her a lot."

"Me too," Dad said. In the moonlight, Chloe could see him smile. "I'm glad you feel that way."

55

"But Sandy is—she's—she's impossible!" Chloe burst out. "It's like I never know which Sandy I'm going to get. The friendly one? Or the unfriendly one? The one who laughs at my jokes? Or the one who acts like I don't even exist? I don't even know what to say or how to be around her. I'm, like, *dreading* spending the whole day with her tomorrow. It's totally exhausting!"

Dad waited patiently until Chloe finished. Then he wrapped his arm around her shoulders. "This is one of those times when I can't tell if you want advice or you just need to vent," he told her.

"I'm not sure," Chloe admitted. "Maybe both?"

"Well, my best dad advice for you is to continue on as you have," he said. "Be yourself. You know—that funny, kind, clever Chloe that the whole world loves."

Not the whole *world*, Chloe thought as she stirred her tea.

"Jessica thinks you're amazing," Dad said, which made Chloe feel better—a little better, anyway. "We both appreciate how hard you've been trying with Sandy. Don't think we haven't noticed.

"This is a big deal for all of us," Dad continued, "and I'll be honest—it's not as easy as I expected it would be. It's bringing up a lot of emotions for everybody—especially Sandy."

"Why are *her* feelings more important than everybody else's?" Chloe asked. "I get that it was stupid for me to hope she'd be my sis—I mean, my friend. But would it kill her to, I don't know, stop making me feel like a speck of dirt? It's like she came into this weekend hoping it would fail—and ready to do everything she could to make sure it did."

"What do you mean?"

Chloe already wished she could take the words back, but it was too late now. Besides, she wasn't in the habit of keeping secrets from Dad, and she wasn't about to start because of Sandy.

"Sandy says her parents are getting back together," Chloe said, hesitating a little. It was only when she heard those words aloud that she realized they could really, really hurt her dad's feelings. And Chloe was pretty sure that Sandy was wrong...but what if she was actually right?

Luckily, Dad didn't seem fazed.

"Poor Sandy," Dad said. "I remember when I felt that way."

Chloe scrunched up her face in confusion. "About *Jessica*?" she asked.

Dad's booming laugh echoed through the room. "No! About my own parents," he said. "They divorced when I was nine years old, remember? I was certain that they'd get back together. I mean, how could they not? We were a family, and family is forever."

Chloe was very quiet. She knew that Nana and Poppy were divorced, but they'd been divorced for so long that she'd never really thought about it...or what it would've been like for her dad when he was a boy.

"A few years passed—but I didn't give up hope. Then Poppy started dating Mimi, and Nana started dating Grandpa Dave, and when Poppy and Mimi got engaged they invited Nana and Dave to their wedding. That's when I realized that Poppy and Nana *definitely* weren't going to get back together. But that didn't mean that our family was ruined or broken. It was just different. Bigger. And now I can't imagine it any other way."

"Do you think Sandy will ever feel that way?" Chloe asked.

"I hope so," Dad replied. "It's pretty exhausting to hold on to so much anger and pain. But it's still early for Sandy to adjust to all the changes in her life. Jessica says we should give her time...which is pretty much all we can do."

Chloe sipped her tea in silence, thinking about what her dad had said. In all the times she'd thought about this trip, it had never occurred to her that Sandy would be struggling with her own issues. *If Sandy can't try to make the trip work*, Chloe decided, *then I'll have to try twice as hard.*

Chapter 5

When Chloe awoke the next morning, she pulled back the curtain to peek outside. The sun was shining with such dazzling light that Chloe had to shield her eyes just from glancing out the window. *I need my sunglasses more here than I needed them at the beach last summer,* she thought. Luckily, Chloe had a brand-new pair of ski goggles for their outdoor adventures. Dad had surprised her with them as an early Christmas present.

Remembering that the lines for snow tubing would be long, Chloe picked out her warmest clothes, from her fleece-lined jeans to her chunky cable-knit sweater. Then she got dressed and bounded into the kitchen, where Dad was finishing his coffee.

"Morning, sleepyhead!" Dad said. "I was just about to wake you up. You don't want to laze away the day."

"Are you even kidding?" Chloe pretended to be outraged. "*I'm* dressed and ready to go. You're still in your pajamas!"

Dad glanced down at his plaid pj's and pretended to slap himself in the forehead. "Right! I *knew* I was forgetting something!" he joked.

Chloe gave him a little push toward the door. "You go get dressed. I'll feed Charlie and give him his medicine. Then we can—oh!"

"What's wrong?" Dad asked.

"I almost forgot about *my* breakfast!" Chloe said as her face fell. "So much for beating the snow-tubing line. Eating in the restaurant will take ages."

"No worries," Dad told her. "There's a breakfast bar up at the lodge, and they make custom breakfast burritos. We can grab some to go and eat them on the way to snow tubing."

"Awesome!" Chloe cheered. "What are we waiting for?"

"Bet you I can get dressed before you finish with Charlie," Dad said. "On your mark, get set—"

"Go!" they said at the same time.

While Dad got ready, Chloe sped through the rest of Charlie's morning routine. Pill in mouth! Food in bowl! Leash on collar! Jaunt around the cabin! Chloe and Charlie got back to Sugar Plum Cottage just as Dad, all bundled up, stepped out the front door.

"Tie!" Chloe and Dad yelled at the same time.

Chloe's eyes gleamed as she brought Charlie inside. "Rematch," she announced. "Race you to the lodge!"

"Oh, you're on," Dad replied. "On your mark, get set, *go!*"

By the time Chloe and Dad reached the lodge, they were laughing so hard they could barely run anymore. The aromas from the breakfast bar filled the lobby, making Chloe's mouth water. She noticed Sandy standing near the line and hurried over to join her.

"Sandy! Hey!" Chloe exclaimed. "Can you believe this breakfast bar? They'll wrap anything you want in a pancake and call it a breakfast burrito. Scrambled eggs! Bacon! French toast sticks! Anything!"

"Wow," Sandy said. She didn't bother to glance up from her phone. Chloe wasn't even sure that she'd been listening.

"Are you...hungry?" Chloe asked.

Sandy frowned, swiped at the screen, and frowned harder. Chloe started to worry. What if Sandy had gotten a message with bad news? What if it was something from her dad?

"Hey," Chloe said, tapping Sandy's arm. "Is everything okay? You seem upset."

When Sandy glanced up, Chloe could see the anxiety in her green eyes. "Look at this," she said, thrusting her phone at Chloe.

Chloe took the phone from Sandy and scanned the screen. A weather app was open, and it showed a gray cloud hovering over the date—December 23. Not just a gray cloud, but a gray cloud with snowflakes.

"Snow?" Chloe squealed. "It's going to *snow*?"

"That's what everyone is talking about in the lobby," Sandy said. "They were going on and on about it. Apparently the roads get really bad in the mountains and sometimes they get closed for *days*!"

Chloe was about to squeal again—she couldn't think of anything more unexpected and exciting than getting snowed in at the lodge for Christmas—but the look on Sandy's face stopped her just in time.

"Are you okay?" Chloe asked.

"No," Sandy replied. "I don't want to get stuck here! We're supposed to leave first thing tomorrow morning. What if this freak snowstorm shows up and we can't get out of here?"

It's not exactly a freak snowstorm when it happens in the middle of December, Chloe thought, but she didn't want to make Sandy even madder. "I'm sure everything would be just fine," Chloe tried to reassure her. "I bet the lodge has generators and enough food to last for several days. It's been around for decades; this isn't the first time they've had to deal with a snowstorm."

Anger flashed through Sandy's eyes. "You don't get it," she said through gritted teeth. "I'm not worried about how we'll survive if we get snowed in. I want to avoid getting snowed in at all!"

"Well, I mean, that's totally out of our hands," Chloe said. "We can't exactly control the weather."

"Yes, thank you, I know that," Sandy said. "But we could leave early. We could pack up and check out this afternoon instead of tomorrow, and then we could get home before the storm hits."

Before Chloe could respond, Sandy grabbed her arm. "Would you help me?" she asked. "I already asked my mom if we could leave, and she said no, but maybe if we *both* ask her—she thinks you're totally amazing—she'd probably listen to you, or you could ask your dad and I could ask my mom again—"

At first, Chloe was so stunned she didn't know what to say.

Then she found her voice. "No," she said. "No way."

"But—"

"I don't want to leave early," Chloe said firmly, just to make sure there was no doubt about where she stood. And it was true. Chloe had been looking forward to this trip for months. Sandy had done enough to try to derail it. Chloe wasn't about to let her end it early—not for a little snowstorm that might not even happen.

"I've been excited about this trip for so long," Chloe continued. "And that includes obsessing over the weather forecast. I've checked it every single night for a month. Even last night, there was no snow in the forecast. Big storms usually show up, like, days in advance. I'm not even convinced we'll get any snow."

"But you don't *know*," Sandy said stubbornly.

"Nobody does!" Chloe exclaimed. "But I do know this—I'm not going to miss the big party tonight for a few flurries that may or may not fall. Now, I'm really hungry. Do you want to hit the breakfast bar with me or should I go by myself?"

Sandy didn't say anything, but she did move into the line next to Chloe. The girls were quiet as they waited to order breakfast. Chloe wanted to say something—anything—to fix things, but she didn't know where to begin. There were a ton of questions whirling through her mind.

Why does Sandy want to leave so badly? she wondered. *Is she really having such a terrible time that she wants to leave early? Is it me? Does she hate being stuck with me?*

If only she and Sandy knew each other better, Chloe might have found the courage to ask. But they were like strangers. *And strangers,* Chloe thought, *don't have any reason to make up when they don't get along to begin with.*

But it was Christmas—the one time of year when everybody was supposed to be filled with joy and love. It was a season for miracles. A time when *anything* could happen.

And that was enough to give Chloe hope.

❄ ❄ ❄

During the long wait for snow tubing, Chloe kept up such a steady stream of chatter that her throat started to feel dry from talking so much. It was worth it, though. Anything was better than the awkward silence that happened when Sandy refused to participate in the conversation. And once Chloe got everyone started on sharing their favorite Christmas memories, even Sandy couldn't resist listening in— and laughing along to the funny stories.

"How about you?" Jessica asked Dad. "What's your best Christmas story?"

"So hard to pick," Dad said, shaking his head. "Here's a favorite, though. Chloe was three years old—"

"*Dad!*" Chloe groaned. "Do you have to tell this one?"

"But, sweetie, it was one of the best Christmases of all time," Dad said. "You have nothing to be embarrassed about."

"Fine. Go ahead," Chloe said, sighing. Her cheeks were already turning pink.

"I'd decided to get Chloe a puppy for Christmas," Dad began. "Of course, it would've been impossible to keep a puppy secret...and I really wanted her to be surprised when she woke up on Christmas morning. So our neighbors kept the puppy for me, and they played with him first thing Christmas morning, to tire him out."

"Wait—so the puppy was Charlie?" asked Jessica.

"Yes, but he didn't have a name yet," Dad said. "So anyway, early in the morning, our neighbors put a big bow around Charlie's neck and nestled him in a basket under the tree. He was so tired from playing that he fell sound asleep."

"Those are some good neighbors," Jessica said. Then she turned to Chloe. "How come you didn't want your dad to tell this story? It's sweet."

"Just wait," Chloe said. But she didn't *really* mind that Dad was telling it.

"Anyway, little Chloe wakes up, and we rush downstairs to open presents," Dad said, "and I'm really excited because I know she's going to be so happy when she sees the puppy, but she passes right by him and starts opening a present instead. And I'm thinking, what's wrong with this kid? There's a *puppy* under the *Christmas tree*!

"Anyway, I try to nudge her over to the puppy, and then she sneezes, which wakes up puppy Charlie, who starts yipping, and Chloe starts screaming! It turns out she thought the sleeping puppy was actually a stuffed animal, and that her *sneeze* brought him to life! So Chloe spent Christmas either playing with puppy Charlie or sneezing on her other toys in hopes that she could bring them to life, too!"

As Dad finished the story, Jessica and Sandy were laughing so hard that people turned to look at them. Even Chloe had to join in the laughter.

"That's one of the best Christmas stories I've ever heard," Jessica said, wiping her eyes. "Sneezing on your toys!"

"Yes, I know, I'm hilarious," Chloe said with a grin. "Glad I could bring so much joy and amusement to your day!"

When they finally reached the front of the line, Chloe turned to Sandy. "You can go first," she told her.

Sandy shook her head. "You were first in line," she said.

Chloe did a funny hop-skip so that she was standing behind Sandy. "Not anymore!" she sang out.

Sandy hesitated before she suddenly ducked behind Chloe. "You're up!" she cried.

The attendant sighed. "You two done?" he asked. "There's a line."

"Sorry!" Chloe exclaimed. She prodded Sandy. "Seriously, you go," she insisted. "I'll be right behind you."

"Okay," Sandy finally gave in. "See you on the other side!"

Chloe watched, her heart pounding with expectation, as Sandy settled into the squishy black tube. The attendant gave her a strong push, and *whoosh!* Sandy careened down the slope. Just before she disappeared from view, Chloe caught a glimpse of Sandy's face, which radiated pure joy.

Yes! Chloe thought, pumping her fist. *Christmas magic in action!*

Then it was Chloe's turn. She plunked down onto the bouncy rubber tube and had just a half moment of second thoughts—the track seemed *really* steep all of a sudden—before the attendant gave her a firm push. And—

Whoosh!

Chloe zipped down the track, shrieking with glee as the tube flew over the bumps and dips. It was way more fun than she had expected!

As she reached the bottom of the hill, Chloe leaned a little too far to the left. Instead of gliding to a stop, her tube slammed into the snowbank on the side of the track, sending a cloud of soft powder into the air. Sandy was waiting for her nearby; she hurried over and held out her hands to help Chloe up.

"That—was—*awesome!*" Chloe exclaimed, trying to catch her breath.

"I know!" Sandy replied. She brushed some snow off Chloe's shoulders. "Thanks so much for letting us try tubing. I've always wanted to go."

Chloe's eyes sparkled with mischief. "Race you back to the line!"

Chapter 6

After lunch, Sandy turned to Chloe. "Do you want to pick what we do next?" she asked.

Chloe tried not to show her surprise. She'd been ready to let Sandy make all the decisions, as long as she didn't insist on leaving early. It would be a small price to pay to keep their trip on track.

"It's only fair," Sandy was saying. "I got to do snow tubing in the morning, so in the afternoon, we can— go skiing, right? You still want to hit the slopes?"

"Actually...not really," Chloe replied. "I'm still kind of cold from tubing. Maybe we could do something inside, where it's nice and warm?"

"That sounds good to me," Jessica said. "There's a few cute stores in town. We could check them out."

Chloe thought of the allowance she'd saved up and smiled. "Shopping could be fun!"

The town was just a short walk away; from the moment Chloe spotted it, she thought it looked like a picture on a Christmas card. The lampposts and stores were decorated with garlands and lights, while the streets were crowded with last-minute shoppers still searching for the perfect present. Everyone was smiling and laughing, and their cheer was contagious. When they passed by some people caroling on the corner, Dad even paused to join in. If they had been home, Chloe probably would've died of embarrassment—but here, it seemed like a totally normal thing to do.

Sandy suddenly grabbed Chloe's arm. "I know where we're going," she said, pointing at a store across the street. The cherry-red awning read PET PALACE.

"Is that some kind of fancy pet store?" Chloe asked. "Lead the way!"

"Mom, can we go check it out?" Sandy asked Jessica.

"Sure!" Jessica replied. "Let's all meet back here in half an hour."

"Have fun, girls," Dad added. "And stay together!"

Inside the Pet Palace, there were glass cases filled with freshly baked dog bones and fish-shaped cat treats. Chloe and Sandy cracked up as they read the different flavors.

"Salmon Supremes, Tuna Treats, Marrow Morsels—*mmm*, delicious!" Chloe joked.

"This is the grossest bakery case I've ever seen," Sandy whispered to Chloe.

"But Charlie and Elsa would love it," Chloe replied. "Too bad Charlie can't enjoy any of it."

"That is too bad," Sandy replied. "At least he doesn't know what he's missing! I might get something for Elsa, though."

"You totally should," Chloe said. While Sandy waited in line, Chloe wandered around the rest of the store. There was a tall Christmas tree that was covered in all sorts of animal ornaments—from peacocks, zebras, and giraffes to cats, dogs, and parakeets. While Chloe was searching for a dog ornament that looked like Charlie, something else caught her eye: an ornament of a gray cat curled up on a pillow. The cat had a long, fluffy tail and bright green eyes. It looked exactly like Elsa!

Chloe didn't even have to think about it. She knew right away that she had to buy the cat ornament for Sandy. She was certain that Sandy would love it!

Chloe glanced around to make sure Sandy wasn't nearby. Luckily, Sandy was still busy in the bakery section, so Chloe hurried over to the register. Just before she paid for the ornament, Chloe noticed a packet of adorable catnip mice in bright colors. It was a total impulse buy, but once Chloe pictured beautiful Elsa pouncing on them, she couldn't resist. When Chloe finished checking out, she slipped the presents into her backpack and wandered over to a display of dog collars. Sandy didn't notice a thing.

"Hey!" Sandy said a few minutes later as she approached Chloe. She held up a pink bakery box tied with gold ribbon. "Wouldn't this be the funniest prank ever? I mean, it looks like real bakery treats."

"Just think, you're expecting chocolate cupcakes—but you get Salmon Supremes instead," Chloe said, laughing. "I love this store. Check out this dog collar!"

Chloe showed Sandy the blue-and-green collar, which had embroidered letters that read DON'T FEED THE BEAST.

"That is hilarious," Sandy said. "Are you going to buy it?"

"Oh—no, I don't think so," Chloe replied. The truth was, she'd spent almost all her money on the presents for Sandy and Elsa.

"Let's go back and meet the parents," Sandy said. "My mom almost never lets me go off by myself. I don't want to be late and give her a reason to say no next time."

"I hear that!" Chloe replied. They were almost back at the lamppost when Sandy suddenly gasped.

"My wallet!" Sandy exclaimed. "I left it on the bakery counter!"

"Uh-oh! Let's go back and get it," Chloe replied.

"You stay here," Sandy ordered. "That way you can tell my mom where I am."

"But they told us to stay together," Chloe protested.

Sandy shot her a look. "Just stay here, okay? I'll be fine on my own. And I'll be right back!"

Then she dashed back across the street before Chloe had a chance to argue any more. Chloe sighed in frustration. Just when she thought she and Sandy were getting along, Sandy's attitude shifted back to awful. It was so weird, too, because there were times when Chloe really liked Sandy. Times when she thought they might actually become friends.

What will I tell Dad if he and Jessica get here before Sandy comes back? Chloe wondered.

Luckily, Sandy returned in just a couple minutes.

"Find your wallet?" Chloe asked.

"What? Oh, yeah. It's all good," Sandy said just as Dad and Jessica walked up to them.

"What's good?" Jessica asked as she wrapped her arm around Sandy's shoulders.

"Everything," Sandy replied. "Everything's good. Everything's great! Can we go back to the lodge now? I'm starving."

Chloe's eyes narrowed when Sandy said that everything was great. Did she really mean it?

❄ ❄ ❄

Back at the lodge's restaurant, Jessica snagged a table by the fireplace again and checked her watch. "I think we have just enough time for a cup of cocoa," she said.

"Oh! Can we order the cocoa cart?" Sandy exclaimed, pointing at the menu.

"Pleeeease?" Chloe added.

"Why would we order anything else?" Dad teased them.

"This looks amazing!" Chloe squealed when their server wheeled the cocoa cart to their table. The gold cart was covered with a crisp white tablecloth; on top of it was a tall pitcher of steaming hot chocolate. But the best part was all the little bowls of toppings: whipped cream, marshmallows, miniature candy canes, chocolate shavings, rainbow sprinkles, edible gold stars. There were even tiny glass bottles of different flavored syrups to add—everything from peppermint to hazelnut.

"The custom cocoa of our dreams," Jessica said with a laugh. "I don't know where to begin!"

"I do," Dad replied. "With a little of everything!"

After they had passed around all the different toppings, everyone grew quiet as they sipped their mugs of cocoa. Across the table, Sandy grinned at Chloe, and for a moment, Chloe felt so perfectly and completely happy that she wished she could stop time.

"Oh, it's going to be a doozy!" There was an older man sitting a few tables away from them, and his voice grew louder and louder the more he talked. "I can already tell. There's a certain quality in the air, a frosty foreshadowing, if you will. I don't expect they'll get the roads plowed for a week. Maybe more."

"You've got to love the lodge," Dad said, chuckling. "They even have old-timers who can predict the weather."

Jessica laughed, too, but Sandy's smile disappeared, and she looked away from Chloe as she stared at her phone.

"Mom," Sandy said in a low, urgent voice. "Look

at this! The storm is getting worse. Now we might get six to eight inches overnight!"

"Let me see," Jessica said, frowning as she reached for Sandy's phone. "Hmm. That is more snow than they were predicting this morning."

"We have to leave today," Sandy announced. "We can't get trapped here!"

"Okay, let's not overreact," Jessica said. "It's not exactly a blizzard. I think we'll be fine."

"I bet they've already salted the roads," Dad added. "The plows will be lined up, ready to go as soon as it starts to stick."

"But this morning, I heard somebody saying that the roads get really bad up here," Sandy said. "What if they get all icy and dangerous and the plows can't get through and *we* can't get out?"

"I really don't think that's going to happen," Jessica said. "Besides, I can think of worse things than getting snowed in at the lodge!"

"Are you kidding?" Sandy exclaimed. She sounded even more upset now. "We can't risk it! We need to leave *today*!"

Now Chloe was starting to get upset. So far,

Sandy had gotten her way almost every time. What if she got her way now, too? She had to speak up. She had to say something.

"But what about the party?" Chloe said.

"Who *cares* about the stupid party?" Sandy snapped. "We *can't* get snowed in here!"

"Hey, hey, hey," Dad said soothingly, trying to calm Sandy. "They're used to snow in the mountains. They get big snowstorms all the time up here. They can handle it."

"You don't *know* that!" Sandy shot back. Her words sounded rude, but from where Chloe was sitting, she could see how worried Sandy looked.

Unfortunately, Jessica couldn't.

"Sandy," she said sharply. "That is *enough*."

Everyone turned to look at her, but Jessica's eyes were locked with Sandy's. When she spoke again, her voice was lower—but to Chloe, it almost sounded worse than if she had yelled.

"Since we arrived, your behavior has been appalling," Jessica told her daughter. "Tom and Chloe might have limitless patience for your attitude, but I don't. It stops now, Sandy."

"But—"

"*Now*," Jessica repeated. "Let me be clear: We are not leaving early for a snowstorm that hasn't even started yet. You can either fix your attitude, or you can spend the rest of the trip in your room before we leave *tomorrow*, as planned. Understand?"

Sandy slouched so far down in her seat that her head was barely visible above the table. "Yes," she muttered.

Then Jessica turned to Chloe and Dad. "I'm very sorry about that," she said. "If you'll excuse us, Sandy and I are going to go back to our cottage to get ready for the party."

"Of course," Dad said. He leaned over and gave Jessica a kiss on the cheek. "See you later."

"Bye," Chloe said in a soft voice as Jessica and Sandy walked away from the table.

But she wasn't sure if they even heard her.

Chapter 7

The sun had just finished setting when Dad knocked on Chloe's door. "How's it going in there?" he called through the door. "Are you ready for the party?"

"Almost!" Chloe replied as she put on her sparkly snowflake earrings. Then she opened the door and spun around so that the skirt of her dress flared. "Ta-da! What do you think?"

"Wow!" Dad exclaimed. "You look beautiful, Chloe. So grown-up, I can't believe it!"

Chloe's smile grew even bigger. Then she noticed her dad's tie. "Seriously?" she asked. "You're wearing a light-up tie in the shape of a Christmas tree?"

Dad glanced down at his tie. "Pretty great, isn't it?" he asked. "Check it out—the lights have three different flash settings! And if I push this button, it plays Christmas songs! Want to give it a try?"

Chloe held up her hands. "No thanks," she said. "I'm good. But, ah, Dad...I thought this was, you know, a *fancy* party." *Not a ridiculous-looking-light-up-musical-tie party*, she wanted to add—but Chloe kept that thought to herself.

Dad nodded solemnly at her, but Chloe couldn't miss the amusement in his eyes. "It is," he replied. "That's why I bought such a fancy tie. I remember the lodge's website specifically said 'festive dress encouraged.'"

"Festive, not funny-looking!" Chloe laughed.

There was a knock at the door.

"That must be Jessica and Sandy," Dad said.

"Or maybe just Jessica," Chloe said, remembering the look on Sandy's face that afternoon. She'd been so upset that Chloe wouldn't have been surprised if Sandy had decided to stay in her room for the rest of the trip in protest.

"Jessica texted me a little while ago. She said they're

both definitely coming," Dad replied. "Hope they're as ready to party as we are!"

"I don't know, Dad," Chloe teased him. "When they see that tie, maybe even Jessica will want to go home early!"

"We'll see about that," Dad said. Then he opened the door. "Merry Christmas Eve Eve!"

"Merry Christmas Eve Eve!" Jessica and Sandy replied as they hurried inside.

"*Brrr*," Jessica added, rubbing her arms. "Either my party dress isn't nearly as warm as my snowveralls, or it's gotten a lot colder out there."

"Probably both," Sandy said, deftly stepping around her mom as Dad gave Jessica a quick hug.

That's when Chloe saw it. She would have recognized it anywhere—her perfect party dress. But it wasn't only Chloe who was wearing it.

Sandy was wearing it, too.

The only difference between their dresses was the color. Chloe's dress was cranberry-colored, while Sandy's was a deep, rich green. Beyond that, the dresses were identical. Same swooshy, swirly skirt. Same lacy top with long sleeves. Chloe could just see the edges of them peeking out from the cuffs of Sandy's overcoat.

Sandy noticed their matching dresses at the same time. She slowly shrugged off her overcoat, and that's when Chloe started to worry. *Uh-oh*, she thought. *Is this going to set Sandy off? Is she going to be upset that we're matching at the party? If she gets mad, I can't change my dress! It's the only fancy dress I brought!*

Just then, Sandy started to laugh. "Chloe! You look *amazing*," she said. "I love your style!"

Chloe laughed, too, relieved. "No, stop, *I* love *your* style," she said. "Your dress is perfect."

"No, *your* dress is perfect," said Sandy.

"You two look like the Christmas twins," Dad joked. "Come on, let's head over to the party. I can already tell you'll be the belles of the ball!"

❄ ❄ ❄

The celebration at the lodge was the best party Chloe had ever attended. She ate warm gingerbread cake with cinnamon whipped cream, took a bunch of funny photos with Sandy in the photo booth, and danced to jazzy Christmas tunes until her feet ached.

87

She loved every moment of it...especially seeing Dad and Jessica slow dance to the last song of the night.

After she got home from the party, Chloe remembered that she still had to wrap Sandy's present. She was searching her room for wrapping supplies when she heard Dad call her name.

"What's up?" she called back as she poked her head into the hall.

"You coming for teatime?" he asked.

"Right! Sorry, Dad. I got caught up," Chloe replied. She padded down the hall in her slippers and found Dad bringing a tray with two mugs of tea into the living room. Chloe wrapped her hands around one of the cups and inhaled deeply. "Mmm, peppermint," she said. "Perfect for Christmas Eve Eve!"

"I thought you'd appreciate that," Dad said with a smile. Then he glanced at the clock on the mantel. "Whoa—it's later than I thought. Pretty soon it will be Christmas *Eve*! Drink fast, kiddo. You've got to get to bed or you'll be exhausted tomorrow."

"I'll be okay," Chloe assured him. "Besides, I can always sleep in the car on the drive home."

"Just what I need—a copilot who sleeps on the

job," Dad joked. "So what have you been up to since we got home from the party?"

Chloe grinned at him. "I *guess* I can trust you not to spill the secret," she said. "Stay there—I'll be right back!"

A few minutes later, Chloe returned from her room with the bag from the Pet Palace. "I got a Christmas present for Sandy," she said. "It's not much—but when I saw it in the store, I just knew she had to have it."

Chloe opened the bag and showed Dad the ornament that looked just like Elsa, and the three catnip mice.

For a moment, Dad didn't say anything as he stared at Sandy's present. Chloe shifted uncomfortably on the couch. "Do you—do you think she won't like it?" she asked.

Dad looked up at her. "No, no—I think Sandy will love it," he said quickly. "I was just thinking"—Dad paused to clear his throat—"I was just thinking what a kind thing this was. To spend your money on a gift for someone who hasn't been very kind to you."

Chloe shrugged a little as she glanced away. "It's not a big deal," she mumbled.

"Sometimes little things, little acts of kindness, are the biggest deal," Dad told her. "Especially to someone who's hurting. Whose pain is making her act out in all kinds of unpleasant ways."

"But Sandy had fun at the party, didn't she?" Chloe asked.

Dad nodded. "Yes, I think so," he replied. "At least, I hope so. And I'm glad the trip will be ending with a happy memory for us all to take home." He reached over and picked up one of the catnip mice, dangling it by the ribbon tail. "And for Elsa it seems like the fun will be just beginning!"

Chloe started to laugh but stopped abruptly.

"Hey—what's wrong?" asked Dad.

"The mouse's tail is made of ribbon," she realized. "Ribbon! It can make cats really sick if they eat it!"

Dad tugged on the toy mouse's tail. "It seems pretty firmly attached," he told her.

"I don't want to take any chances," Chloe said. "I'll have to cut off their tails—even though they're really cute. Better to be safe than sorry."

She scooped the catnip mice into her palm and

carried them into the kitchen. *Snip, snip, snip.* Just like that, the tails were off—and the toys were safe for Elsa to enjoy. They were stuffed so full of catnip that Chloe had a feeling she would love them!

Suddenly, Chloe yawned so big her jaw hurt. In that moment, she realized how exhausted she was: from snow tubing to shopping to dancing, Chloe's day had been nonstop. Wrapping Sandy's gift, she decided, could wait until morning. *It will be one last thing to do before we say goodbye to the lodge,* she decided. Between Sandy's attitude and Charlie's illness, the trip had been a lot more stressful than Chloe had anticipated, but she was still a little sad that it was almost over.

At the same time, she was ready to go home.

Chapter 8

"Chloe?"

She could hear Dad calling her name, but his voice was so soft. It almost sounded far away. Chloe mumbled something in response as she rolled over and pulled the blanket over her head.

"Chloe? Chloe! Wake up, Chloe!"

Dad was shaking her shoulder and speaking louder now. Chloe couldn't have slept through it if she tried.

"Too early," she groaned. "Just wanna sleep a little…"

"Chloe, honey, there's been a big storm," Dad said.

Chloe's eyes snapped open as she bolted upright in bed. "Are you serious?" she gasped. "How much snow?"

"Two feet, maybe three," Dad said. "The drifts are so high it's hard to tell exactly how much fell overnight."

"You've *got* to be kidding!" Chloe cried as she raced over to the window. She pulled back the curtain and gasped when she saw the winter wonderland outside. Though a pale, eerie light reflected off the snow-covered surfaces, Chloe could see that the snow was still falling pretty heavily. The world outside the cabin was almost unrecognizable.

"Oh no," she said, turning to face Dad. "Sandy is going to freak out!"

"Yes," he said, glancing at a text message on his phone. "Apparently, she already has."

"What if we're stuck?" Chloe wondered. "We're not stuck up here, right? They plowed the roads, didn't they? Didn't they?"

"I...have no idea," Dad admitted. "Honestly, from here I can barely even see the roads. It's not white-out conditions...but it was probably pretty close overnight."

"What are we going to do?" Chloe asked.

"That's why I had to wake you up," Dad told her. "We've got to get over to the lodge and find out our options. Charlie's had his breakfast and medicine, so go ahead and get dressed—bundle up, lots of layers—and let's go. Jessica and Sandy will meet us there."

After Chloe got dressed, she and Dad trudged through the waist-deep snow. It was dense, heavy snow—great for building a snowman, or even a snow fort—but Chloe knew that the same qualities that made it perfect to play in would make their travel home especially tricky.

"How was Charlie when you took him out?" Chloe asked as they approached the lodge. "Is he still feeling okay?"

"Yes, he's fine," Dad said. "I think his upset stomach the other day was just a fluke. He ate every bite of his breakfast. And speaking of breakfast, maybe you and Sandy can get something to eat while Jessica and I figure out what to do."

"I'm not sure Sandy will have much appetite," Chloe said as they walked into the lobby. "She's probably going to be too upset to eat." After a moment of searching, Chloe spotted Jessica. "Dad! I see them," Chloe said, pointing at the long line snaking toward the reservations desk.

"Oh, good—they're almost at the front of the line," Dad said. "Let's find out what's going on."

As Chloe and her father squeezed into line beside Jessica and Sandy, Chloe noticed how relieved Jessica looked to see Dad, even though the worried expression never left her face. "Morning," she said. "Quite a winter wonderland out there, isn't it?"

"Spare me," Sandy said, shaking her head in disgust.

Dad and Jessica exchanged a glance. "As you can guess, I'm not very popular right now," Jessica said, still trying to make light of the situation.

"I can't believe you think this is funny!" Sandy snapped. "It's Christmas Eve, and we're *stuck* here and you keep making jokes!"

"Lower your voice, please," Jessica said. Then she turned back to Dad. "We haven't even reached the front of the line, but from what I gather, the roads are pretty much impassable. And they don't expect the plows to make it up here for at least three or four days."

"Three or four *days*?" Chloe exclaimed. Back home, they'd never gotten snowed in for more than a day or two.

Jessica nodded grimly. "The plows take care of the city first, then the suburbs, and make it into the mountains last," she explained. "But maybe that was just a rumor. Maybe when we get to the front of the line, we'll find out that—"

"Next!" a young woman called.

Dad put his hand on Jessica's shoulder. "I think that's us," he said.

The woman behind the desk greeted them with a smile as bright as her shiny gold name tag, which read MARA. "Good morning!" she chirped. "How can I help you?"

"We're supposed to be checking out today—but

we're not sure we can leave," Jessica began. "When do you expect the roads to be cleared?"

"Three to four days, at least," the woman replied. "And that's if they don't freeze overnight. Then it could be a week."

"A week?" Sandy cried in dismay.

Mara nodded. "But don't worry—we're happy to extend your reservation at a lowered rate," she said. "And on the plus side, it looks like we'll definitely be having a white Christmas here at the lodge!"

"Mom," Sandy said urgently, pulling on Jessica's hand. "We can't stay longer—we have to go home. We—"

"Sandy, I can't do this right now," Jessica said shortly. But Sandy wouldn't stop.

"You *promised* we'd be home for Christmas," she said—and this time, Chloe noticed that there was no anger in Sandy's voice. Just a desperate, quivery hope. "Please, Mom, *please*, you *promised*—"

"You go ahead and talk to Sandy," Dad said to Jessica as he stepped up to the counter. "I'll handle this."

"Thank you," Jessica said gratefully as she guided Sandy over to a small alcove.

"Sorry about that, Mara," Dad said. "What do we need to do to extend our reservation?"

"Last name?" Mara asked.

"Warner and Martinez," Dad replied.

Mara's long nails went *clack-clack-clack* on the keyboard. As Mara peered at the screen, her smile faded.

Uh-oh, Chloe thought. *That can't be good.*

"Well, I have good news and bad news," Mara finally said. "The bad news is that your cabins have been rented out to a party that's already arrived. But the *good* news is that we'll be happy to accommodate you in rooms in the lodge! And we can send someone to bring your luggage up." Mara smiled brightly again.

"Thank goodness," Dad said. "I don't know what we would've done with two adults, two girls, a cat, and a dog—"

Just like that, Mara's smile went out again, as if someone had flicked a light switch. "Pets?" she said.

"Oh, dear. I'm so sorry, but pets are only allowed in the cabins. Rooms in the lodge are strictly pet-free."

For a moment, Dad was at a loss for words. "But—our pets are already here," he said. "What are we supposed to do? Leave them in the snow?"

"Dad!" Chloe cried indignantly. She didn't care what the policy was—there was no way she'd leave Charlie out in the cold!

"I'm very sorry, sir," Mara replied. "But we simply can't have pets in the lodge, for the comfort of all our guests."

Dad ran his hand through his hair, making it stand up funny, and that's when Chloe realized how stressed out he really was. "Is there, ah, some sort of boarding facility nearby?" he asked.

"Not that you could reach on these roads, I'm afraid," Mara said. "So . . . do you want me to transfer your reservation to the lodge? Or will you be checking out as originally scheduled?"

"Dad, we can't—" Chloe began urgently.

"I know, sweetie," he said. "Just let me think for—wait! If the roads aren't passable, then the people who have reservations for our cottages won't be able to make it."

"Unfortunately, they're already here," Mara said. "They'll be checking in as soon as you've checked out."

"So...you're telling me that there's nothing you can do for us?" Dad asked. "We either take rooms with no arrangements for our pets, or we all check out and—what? Sleep in our cars?"

"I'm sorry, sir," Mara said. "We'll do our best to find a place for your entire family, but we have quite a few guests and reservation extensions to arrange. We'll do everything we can."

Dad sighed in frustration. "Let me speak to the rest of my family," he said. "I'll be right back."

Chloe trailed after Dad, her mind swirling with too many thoughts and emotions to process at once. The storm—being snowed in—losing the cottages— no place for Charlie and Elsa—and now Dad had used the word *family* to describe Jessica and Sandy? Were his feelings for Jessica even stronger now, despite all the drama of the weekend? Were Chloe's most secret wishes about to come true? But—if they did—how would she handle Sandy on a full-time basis? Even their pets didn't get along!

"Tom," Jessica said, "what's the latest?"

"It's not great news," he began. Chloe watched Sandy's face as Dad explained everything. She got very pale at first, and then her cheeks grew pink and her eyes flashed with anger.

"This just gets worse and worse," Sandy snapped. "If you think for even one minute that I'm just going to let Elsa sleep in our freezing-cold car—"

"Nobody's suggesting that," Dad interrupted her.

Sandy whirled around to face him. "How did these other guests even get here?" she demanded. "If we're stuck *in*, why aren't they stuck *out*?"

Dad glanced at Jessica and cleared his throat. "I assume that they arrived last night and stayed at the lodge or nearby—before the storm hit," he said.

"Oh, so they planned ahead?" Sandy asked sarcastically. "If only we had, I don't know, some kind of special technology that could, like, predict big snowstorms!"

Chloe would've laughed if everything wasn't so serious.

"That was pretty smart of them to travel *before* the storm," Sandy continued. "If only we could've—"

"That's enough," Jessica said sharply. "There's no point in saying I told you so. We have to—"

"Sandy's right," Dad spoke up.

Everyone turned to look at him, but his eyes were locked on Sandy.

"I'm sorry, Sandy," he said. "You tried to warn us, but we were so determined to make this getaway work just the way we planned that nobody listened. Your mom and I should've been more responsible, and I apologize for my poor judgment."

For a moment, no one knew what to say. Then Sandy looked away and shrugged. "Whatever. It's fine," she said.

It wasn't fine—they all knew it was very far from fine—but she came pretty close to accepting Dad's apology.

And that, Chloe knew, was a start.

"I can't turn back the clock and get us on the road last night, before the snow," Dad said. "And I can't get us back to our own homes for Christmas. But I'm going to do everything I can to find us a place to stay—and when I say *us*, I mean all of us, Charlie and Elsa included. They're not just pets. They're family members. Where we go, they go."

"How?" Chloe asked. "They're banned from the lodge and there aren't any cabins available."

"The lodge isn't the only hotel in the Poconos," Dad said. "We might not be able to get *home*, but we can probably make it down the road to another resort. Excuse me—I'm going to make some calls."

Chloe's heart swelled with pride. *Dad is the best*, she thought. No matter what went wrong, he was always ready to fix it.

Now all she could do was cross her fingers—and hope for the best.

Chapter 9

"Excuse me!"

Chloe turned around as an older couple hurried over to them.

"I'm sorry, but we couldn't help overhearing," the woman said. "Do you need a cabin? For your pets?"

"Yes!" Chloe exclaimed, glancing over at Jessica. "We have a dog and a cat and they can't come in the lodge—"

"Why, we'd be happy to give you our cabin and stay in the lodge instead," the man said.

"Really?" Jessica asked in disbelief. "You'd do that?"

"Of course we would, dear!" the woman said, patting Jessica's arm. "We don't mind giving up a cabin so your poor little fur babies have a nice warm place to stay."

"And staying in the lodge isn't exactly chopped liver," the man joked.

"Thank you!" Chloe cried. "Thank you *so* much!"

The woman smiled indulgently at her. "You're welcome," she replied. "We booked the Mistletoe, and I think you're going to love it! We stayed there last winter, too. Now, it's on the small size, so it will be a little cozy for a family of four, but I'm sure sisters like you won't mind sharing a room!"

"We're—" Sandy began, but Jessica quickly cut her off.

"The Mistletoe is where we've been since Saturday morning!" Jessica said.

"Even better!" the woman exclaimed, clapping her hands in delight. "Now you won't have to pack up and move! Run along and fetch your father, girls, so you can tell him the good news. We'll get these reservations straightened out so that we can all start celebrating. After all, it's Christmas Eve!"

"I'll tell Dad," Chloe quickly volunteered before Sandy could say anything. She knew he'd be glad to hear that they could stay in a cottage after all—but now that Chloe's immediate sense of relief had passed, the reality of the situation was starting to sink in. Mistletoe Cottage was smaller than the one where Chloe and her dad had stayed. It would be a tight fit under the best of circumstances—but they'd be cramming in there with a dog and a cat who hated each other. *And Sandy*, Chloe thought, *who kind of hates me.*

❅ ❅ ❅

A short while later, Dad and Chloe carried their suitcases over to Mistletoe Cottage. Chloe kept a tight hold on Charlie's leash as he frolicked in the snow. *Hope he gets out some of that energy before he sees Elsa again*, Chloe thought. Then she remembered that Elsa would be staying in Sandy's room now that Dad would be back at their cottage.

Jessica swung open the door before they were halfway down the path. Chloe had a feeling that she'd been watching for them.

"Welcome!" Jessica called out. "Come on in from the cold!"

Inside the entryway, Chloe sniffed the air as she stomped the snow off her boots. "Mmm, something smells good," she said. She unhooked Charlie's leash and hung it on the peg by the door.

"Sandy and I made cocoa," Jessica said. "We thought you'd need to warm up after lugging your suitcases through the snow."

Just then, Sandy appeared in the doorway to the living room, with Elsa trailing behind her. Sandy could've reached down to scoop Elsa into her arms.

But she didn't.

Chloe wished she hadn't unhooked Charlie's leash so soon. But it was too late. He was free—and Elsa was just a few feet away. Chloe's breath caught in her throat. If Charlie charged at Elsa again—even worse, if he accidentally *hurt* her—

But, to Chloe's amazement, Charlie seemed to have learned his lesson. He approached Elsa cautiously, keeping his body close to the ground and his tail low. From all the dog-care books she'd read,

Chloe recognized the pose instantly: Charlie was showing Elsa that she was the boss.

Charlie moved toward Elsa. Everyone watched—and no one moved. Elsa sat very still, watching him through her bright green eyes.

It's working, Chloe thought. *They're not fighting! They're getting to know each other! They're—*

Elsa's paw was a blur of gray as she lashed out at Charlie. Chloe didn't need to see her claws to know they were out. Charlie's whimper of pain—and the way he scurried behind the couch to hide—told her everything she needed to know.

"Charlie!" Chloe cried.

"Oh, Elsa." Jessica sighed in exasperation.

Sandy shrugged. "You can't blame Elsa for defending herself," she said.

Chloe's temper flared—and she only felt angrier when she noticed the specks of bright red blood on Charlie's muzzle. "Charlie didn't even do anything this time!" she said.

"Let's all just—" Dad began. Then his face scrunched up and he sneezed loudly. And again. And again!

"Okay, that's it," Jessica announced. "Sandy, please take Elsa to your room, like we discussed."

"But—"

"Nope," Jessica cut her off. "She's making Tom sneeze and she attacked Charlie. She's lost her living room privileges for the rest of the trip."

"I can—*achoooo!*—take some—*achoooo!*—allergy meds," Dad tried to say.

"Sandy. *Now,*" Jessica said—in a voice that meant business.

Without another word, Sandy bent down to pick up Elsa. Then she disappeared down the hall. The *slam* of her door made the little cabin shake.

"I'm happy to try the medicine," Dad said, wiping his watery eyes.

"It looks like you'll need to try it even if Elsa's in a different room," Jessica said, looking concerned. "I'm so sorry, Tom, I'm sure her fur is everywhere."

"It's not your fault," Dad told her. "It's not anyone's fault."

"Come on—I'll get you a glass of water," Jessica said as she moved toward the kitchen. "How about you, Chloe? I bet you'd like some cocoa."

"Definitely," Chloe replied—but even she could hear that her voice sounded odd. It was strained and hollow, which was a pretty good reflection of how she felt inside. Just a couple days ago, she'd had such high hopes for this trip. Chloe had never dreamed that it would lead to the worst Christmas ever. It wasn't even the fact that there wouldn't be presents or any of the special traditions from home. No, it was all the bad feelings. Jessica and Sandy were obviously having a hard time. Sandy seemed miserable beyond words. Even Elsa and Charlie couldn't get along for five minutes!

It doesn't have to be this way, Chloe thought miserably. But at this point, it would take a Christmas miracle to save the holiday.

On the way to the kitchen, though, Chloe noticed Elsa's food bowl. In her anger, Sandy must have forgotten to grab it. Chloe was about to walk past it when she suddenly stopped. An idea—no, a plan—was slowly starting to unfurl in her mind.

What would I be doing if it were just Dad and me right now? she thought. *We'd play in the snow.*

Probably build a big snowman and then have an even bigger snowball fight. And drink tons of cocoa, and play games, and have Christmas Eve tea. And it would feel like Christmas because we were together and having so much fun.

Even though things were tense, Chloe realized, she could still do her part to make Christmas special. She didn't have to let Sandy's grumpiness or Jessica's worrying or anything else get in the way of a special snowbound Christmas.

I'll ask Jessica to keep the cocoa warm for me, Chloe decided. *Because first I want to play in the snow! And—and maybe Sandy will, too!* Chloe remembered the way Sandy had laughed with glee during snow tubing. Anybody who had that much fun in the snow would definitely be up for a snowball fight. Or maybe even building a snow fort! The possibilities were endless…but Chloe wouldn't know unless she asked.

Impulsively, Chloe picked up Elsa's food bowl and hurried over to Sandy's room. She was so excited she didn't even knock.

"Hey! Sandy! Do you—" Chloe began. But when she realized what was happening, the words stuck in her throat.

Sandy was curled up in a ball on her bed, and even from the doorway Chloe could see the wet streaks of tears on her cheeks. Every few seconds, her shoulders shook with a silent sob. Elsa had abandoned her favorite spot on the pillow and was perched right by Sandy's head. From the look of things, though, not even her beloved kitty could make Sandy feel better.

When she saw Sandy suffering like that, all Chloe could think of was how much she wanted to help. She closed the door and sat on the end of the bed. "Hey, hey, don't cry," she said. "We don't have to let a storm ruin our Christmas! It will be like—like an adventure! And we can play in the snow and watch movies and bake cookies. I promise everything is going to be okay. We can make it okay!"

Sandy sat up and stared at Chloe with tear-filled eyes. "You really don't get it, do you?" she asked. "I thought you were just pretending, but you're not, are you? You don't get it at all."

Chloe had no idea what Sandy was talking about. "I guess not," she said. "Do you want to tell me?"

"This isn't some magical snowbound adventure for me," Sandy snapped. "So no matter what you say, I'm not going to be all, yay, let's frolic in the snow and sing carols by candlelight. Getting stuck here means I won't get to see my dad on Christmas. Do you have any idea what that feels like? Here's a clue. It's basically the worst feeling in the world. So *excuse me* if I can't fake it and pretend that everything is so amazing. But you go ahead. Have your amazing snowy Christmas with your dad and my mom. That's what you've wanted since we got here, isn't it? Everything's working out just the way you wanted! You must be so happy."

Chloe stood there, frozen, until Sandy finished speaking. Even then, Sandy's words seemed to hang in the air, reverberating like a bell that couldn't be unrung.

All Chloe wanted to do was escape from Sandy's room...and Sandy's rage. But she wouldn't just slink away in silence. Not when she'd done nothing wrong. It wasn't easy, but at last, Chloe found her voice.

"None of this makes me happy," she said. "None of it."

Then, with as much dignity as she could muster, she walked out of Sandy's room, closing the door behind her.

Where to go, where to go? Mistletoe Cottage was stupidly small—Chloe couldn't believe she'd ever thought it was cute and cozy. There was no privacy, none! Dad and Jessica were in the kitchen, with that big open window into the living room. No matter where Chloe went, it was only a matter of time before Dad and Jessica realized that something was wrong. She longed to escape to Sugar Plum Cottage, but another family was probably already in there.

I wish we hadn't gotten snowed in, Chloe thought miserably. *I wish we hadn't come at all.*

Chapter 10

But it was too late now. Chloe would just have to make the best of it for the next few days, until the snow melted or the plows could get through. She took a deep, shuddery breath and forced herself to go to the kitchen. *Three's a crowd, but Dad and Jessica will just have to get used to me*, she thought. Tagging along with them would be a thousand times better than being alone with Sandy.

"Hey! Is it cocoa time?" Chloe asked, trying to sound cheerful as always. But her voice faltered a little, which made her chin quiver, and the next thing she knew, her eyes were stinging with tears. She stared off to the side, refusing to meet Dad's or Jessica's gaze, refusing to blink in case the tears spilled out of her eyes despite her best efforts to hide them.

But Chloe couldn't hide it—not from Jessica, and definitely not from Dad.

"I think Charlie could use a walk," Dad said. "Want to join me?"

"Sure," Chloe said. Charlie was curled up on the couch, fast asleep—not whining at the door like he usually did when he wanted to go outside. Dad must've sensed how badly Chloe wanted to escape from Mistletoe Cottage…and Charlie was the perfect excuse.

When Chloe took Charlie's leash off the peg on the wall, his ears twitched. Then he bolted off the couch and scampered over to the door. As Chloe bent down to ruffle his fur, Charlie put his paws on her shoulders and licked her face with his pink tongue. Impulsively, Chloe wrapped her arms around him and gave him a hug. No matter what was wrong, Charlie always knew how to make her feel better.

When they walked outside, the sun was peeking

out from behind the clouds; it wasn't blindingly bright yet, but Chloe could tell that the snow-covered mountainside would be a dazzling sight if the sun kept shining. She took a deep breath and let the frosty air fill her lungs. Nothing had changed—nothing was fixed—but somehow, Chloe started to feel better anyway.

For several minutes, neither one of them said a word. Chloe knew that Dad wasn't going to push her to tell him what had happened. It wasn't his style to pry. But now, after walking through the quiet, peaceful landscape, she felt ready to open up.

"Dad," Chloe began. "I think I know why Sandy has been so upset about the storm."

Then she told him everything. She told him about Sandy's dad, their ruined Christmas plans. All of it.

When Chloe finally finished, a pained expression crossed Dad's face. "I've been wondering if there was something else going on—something Sandy didn't want to tell us," he said. "She was just too upset. It didn't make sense."

"So…she didn't even tell Jessica?" asked Chloe. That was hard for her to understand. If her mom was still alive, Chloe had a feeling she'd tell her *everything*.

"Not that I know of," Dad replied. "I don't know all the details of Jessica's divorce, but she and her ex-husband have a pretty strict policy against discussing the other one with Sandy. They didn't want to trouble her with the problems in their relationship…but maybe they took things a little too far."

"So you think that Sandy felt like she *couldn't* tell her mom?" Chloe guessed.

"I think it's possible," Dad replied. "Which would be a pretty heavy burden for her to carry."

Chloe was quiet as she thought about it. How lonely it must've felt for Sandy, to be missing her dad and dreading Christmas without him—and not be able to tell anyone how she really felt.

"Kiddo, do you mind if we head back to the cabin?" Dad's voice interrupted Chloe's thoughts. "Jessica has been really worried about Sandy. This information might help ease her mind."

"Sure," Chloe said. All of a sudden, she wasn't dreading her return to Mistletoe Cottage. She was ready to try again with Sandy—and in that moment, Chloe realized that she'd gladly try again, and again, and again to mend things with Sandy. Chloe knew that it wasn't her fault; she hadn't done anything wrong. But it seemed clearer than ever that what Sandy really needed—what she needed most of all— was a friend.

Maybe she'd accept Chloe's friendship.

Maybe she wouldn't.

Either way, Chloe was determined to try.

❄ ❄ ❄

Back at Mistletoe Cottage, Chloe and her dad found Jessica humming as she puttered around the kitchen, lining up ingredients on the counter. "Hey there, snowbirds!" she called out cheerfully. "How was your walk?"

"Good!" Chloe replied. "We really wore Charlie out. I think he's ready for a long winter's nap."

"Elsa is in the nap zone, too," Sandy spoke up.

"I guess that's something they have in common after all."

That's when Chloe realized that Sandy was perched on one of the chairs by the fireplace. Her arms were wrapped around her knees, and Chloe could tell from her red-rimmed eyes that Sandy had been crying—a lot. But Sandy managed to smile at Chloe anyway.

And Chloe gratefully smiled in return.

"Oh no!" Jessica cried.

"What's wrong? Did you cut yourself?" Dad asked.

"No, no, I'm fine," Jessica said. "I was just getting ready to make Christmas cookies—it's Christmas Eve and it doesn't smell like Christmas Eve, not without the scent of cookies baking. And the pantry is so well stocked, it's got everything we need, but the fridge…"

"Uh-oh," Dad replied. "What are you missing?"

"Butter," Jessica said, making a face. "There isn't anything I can substitute for it. We don't even have a can of shortening!"

"You know what?" Chloe spoke up. "They must

have lots of butter up at the lodge in the restaurant. I bet they'd give us some if we asked. I've still got my boots on....I can go find out."

Then Chloe had a brilliant idea. She turned to Sandy. "Want to come with me?"

"Um...sure," Sandy said. She looked surprised by the invitation, but not as surprised as Chloe was that Sandy had accepted it.

"Here," Jessica said, hurrying toward Sandy's room. "Let me get your scarf and hat!"

Sandy and Chloe exchanged a smile. They didn't have to say a word for Chloe to know they were thinking the same thing: *Parents!*

"*So obvious,*" Sandy mouthed.

"*Totally,*" Chloe silently replied.

Then they smiled again.

After they were all bundled up, Chloe and Sandy stepped outside. The path to the lodge had been well trampled by then, so it was easier for them to make the journey. Chloe didn't waste any time.

"I want you to know that I'm really sorry we got snowed in," she began. "I didn't realize that us getting snowed in would mean that you couldn't see your dad for Christmas. I mean, no wonder you were so upset! I feel awful about—about everything. I'm definitely not happy about the fact that you won't get to spend Christmas with your dad."

"I know you're not," Sandy said in a small voice. "I don't know why I said that. It was mean, and it wasn't true."

It wasn't exactly an apology, but it inspired Chloe to keep going anyway.

"My mom's been gone for such a long time that I never thought about what it would be like if my parents were divorced instead," Chloe continued. "How hard it must be, to miss your dad and know that he's out there, missing you, too. To worry that he was having a lonely Christmas all by himself, when you should've been there with him."

Chloe wasn't sure if she was saying the right thing—or if her words would make Sandy angry all over again.

When Sandy didn't reply, Chloe felt a sinking feeling in her stomach. But when she glanced at Sandy out of the corner of her eye, she saw that Sandy was wiping her eyes on her mitten.

"I've been the worst," Sandy said. "The *worst*. And you're so, like, *nice* about *everything*...even this stuff with my dad, when you never get to spend Christmas with your mom." Sandy suddenly looked worried. "Sorry!" she said. "I shouldn't have mentioned her."

"Who? My mom?" Chloe asked in confusion.

Sandy nodded.

"You can mention her!" Chloe exclaimed. "I love talking about her."

"Really?" Sandy asked. "It's just—you've never said a word about her. So I told myself not to bring her up."

Chloe smiled a little and shook her head. "No, no, I try not to talk about her because it makes other people feel sorry for me, and then they don't know what to say, and it gets totally awkward," she explained. "But if it doesn't weird you out—"

"Nope," Sandy said. "Not weirded out at all. I hate feeling like I can't talk about my dad when I'm with my mom. It's like he doesn't exist anymore. But he loves Christmas; it's his favorite holiday. That's why I feel so bad that he's going to be all alone."

"My mom loved winter so much," Chloe said, staring at the pine trees dusted with snow. "She used to collect snow globes—I still have them—and my dad told me that she would daydream about wintertime all year long. That's why I wanted to try skiing. It was my mom's favorite sport. So whenever it snows...I think about how excited she would be and then I get excited, too. It...This probably sounds kind of dumb, but it almost makes me feel closer to her."

"That doesn't sound dumb at all," Sandy said. "You must miss her all the time."

"I do," Chloe said honestly. "But my dad says—and I have to believe him—that she'd want me to be happy more than anything else. Even though we can't be together. So I try...for her."

They reached the lodge then, so Chloe pulled open the door and held it for Sandy.

"Thanks," Sandy said.

"No problem," Chloe said, shrugging.

Sandy stopped and looked straight at her. "No, I mean it," she said. "Thank you."

❄ ❄ ❄

When Chloe and Sandy returned to Mistletoe Cottage, they found total pandemonium! Charlie was racing in wild circles around the living room, with Elsa chasing him. There was so much barking and yowling and hissing and shouting that it drowned out the Christmas carols playing on the radio.

"What's going on?" Chloe yelled above all the clamor.

"They just tore in here like this!" Dad yelled back. "And they've been impossible to catch!"

Chloe and Sandy leaped into action. Chloe dodged to the right and crouched down so that she could grab Charlie the next time he raced past, while Sandy dove between the pets in hopes that she could nab Elsa. The sleek gray cat was too quick—and too clever. She jumped over Sandy and just kept going!

"Gotcha!" Chloe cried as she scooped Charlie into her arms and lifted him high above Elsa. Every muscle in his body was trembling, but Chloe couldn't tell if it was from fear or excitement.

"Elsa! Come here right now!" Sandy ordered.

When Elsa realized that Charlie was out of reach, she stalked away, her tail swishing angrily. "Excuse us," Sandy said as she shooed Elsa back to her bedroom. "Someone needs to work on her manners."

"What happened?" Chloe asked again, now that things were calmer. "I thought Elsa was in Sandy's room."

Jessica raised her hand. "It was my fault, I'm afraid," she said. "I think I forgot to close the door when I got Sandy's scarf. Charlie must have wandered in there—maybe he was looking for you, Chloe—and when he did, Elsa went on the attack. Is he okay?"

Chloe examined Charlie, who had stopped trembling. His tongue lolled out of his mouth as she stroked his fur. "Not a scratch on him," she announced.

"Looks like the old boy's still got some speed left in him," Dad joked.

"I think he wants to make friends with Elsa," Chloe said. "Too bad she's not interested!"

Chapter 11

Sandy returned a few minutes later. "Elsa's hiding under my bed, but she'll probably come out as soon as she gets over her embarrassment," she joked. "She's not used to being sent to her room!"

When everyone stopped laughing, Jessica turned to the girls. "How did it go at the lodge? Did you two score some butter?" she asked.

Chloe and Sandy exchanged a grin, then started to laugh. "Yeah, they gave us a little," Chloe joked, holding up a large plastic bucket.

"Is that a *bucket* of *butter*?" Jessica said.

"Yeah, Mom. It's a butter bucket," Sandy said, laughing harder.

"A *ten-pound* bucket of butter," Chloe cried. "For all your Christmas cookie needs!"

"I guess we'll be having cookies for Christmas Eve dinner," said Dad.

"Is that a promise?" Chloe said, making everyone laugh again.

"As well stocked as that pantry is, it's not equipped for Christmas Eve dinner," Jessica said. "That's why I made reservations for us to eat up at the lodge tonight. But enough about dinner—it's time to make some cookies! Crank up the carols, Tom. Christmas is *on*!"

Chloe grinned at Dad. She hadn't seen this side of Jessica before—playful and silly.

"As for you two," Jessica continued, pointing at Chloe and Sandy with a wooden spoon, "come on in here and grab an apron. We've got some serious baking to do before Santa comes down that chimney tonight."

"Right, Mom," Sandy said, rolling her eyes—but

everyone could tell she was playing along. "What are we baking, anyway?"

"Sugar cookies, for sure. Snowballs. Candy-cane cookies. And it's not Christmas without chocolate, so how about some brownies or fudge?" Jessica said. "In fact, why don't we each take a recipe? It'll be like a Christmas cookie bake-off!"

"Can I make the brownies?" Chloe asked. "They're my favorite."

"Only if you let me have a corner piece," Jessica teased her.

"Done!" Chloe said, laughing again. She was halfway to the kitchen when she heard it—a low, soft whine. She turned around and saw Charlie standing by the door.

"Hey, boy," Chloe said. "You want to go out?"

Charlie whined again. Then he barked—a short, sharp bark that caught everyone's attention.

"Guess I need to take Charlie out," Chloe said, reaching for her winter gear yet again.

"Already?" Dad asked. "We just took him for a long walk."

"I know, but…" Chloe shrugged. "He's whining at the door."

"Want me to come with you?" Dad asked.

"That's okay," Chloe replied. "We'll be back soon. You know Charlie doesn't like to stay out in the cold too long."

She hooked Charlie's leash to his collar and stepped outside. Charlie was pulling on the leash so hard that Chloe stumbled a bit. "Whoa, Charlie! I'm coming," she said. Something wasn't right. Charlie didn't usually bark at the door like that—or tug so hard on the leash—

Then it happened. Around the back of Mistletoe Cottage, Charlie got sick again.

"Oh no," Chloe whispered. "Poor Charlie. Poor boy."

There was nothing Chloe could do to make Charlie feel better besides stay with him and say kind things in a soft, soothing voice. Inside, though, her heart was racing, even though Chloe was trying her hardest not to panic. *Something's wrong. Something's wrong with Charlie*, she thought. It was obvious that his gastritis was back. But why? If he hadn't eaten anything unusual—and Chloe was sure that he hadn't—then it could only mean . . .

We've got to get Charlie to the vet, Chloe thought. But they were snowed in! And it was Christmas Eve! Even if their vet back home was open, the office would probably be closed by the time Chloe and Dad could get there.

Chloe forced herself to pause and take a deep breath. *Panicking isn't going to help anything*, she told herself firmly. *I'll walk Charlie for a few more minutes, then tell Dad what's going on. He'll know what to do.*

When Chloe and Charlie got back to the cabin, Chloe carried her pup inside. "Dad!" she called as she walked inside. "Dad! Charlie got sick again!"

"Uh-oh," Dad said as he walked over to them, a look of concern on his face. "What's going on, Charlie boy?"

"He needs to see the vet, don't you think?" Chloe asked, her voice high and tight. "This is the second time in three days! I'm really worried!"

"Well, now, let's stay calm," Dad told her. "Remember when Charlie got really sick? He was much, much worse than he is now."

"I remember," Chloe said.

"And he didn't get sick at all yesterday—remember that?" Dad prompted her.

Chloe nodded.

"So let's just wait and see for a little while," Dad said. "Who knows, maybe it's all the unexpected exertion from his squabbles with Elsa."

"Maybe," Chloe said. She hadn't thought of the connection, but it was true—both times Charlie had been sick after a run-in with Sandy's cat. She glanced over at Charlie, who was curled up in front of the fire, fast asleep. Maybe Dad was right. Maybe Charlie was going to be just fine.

Only time would tell.

"So—how are those cookies coming?" she asked.

"Cookies! Right!" Jessica said, sounding overly cheerful. "Let's get to it!"

Sandy, though, was especially quiet. "I don't really feel like it anymore," she said in a flat voice. "Sorry."

Whoa, Chloe thought. What had happened? She and Charlie had only been outside for fifteen minutes, but in that time, everything had changed.

Jessica sighed and disappeared into the kitchen.

"Dad?" Chloe asked.

"Jessica and Sandy had a fight," he explained. "We should probably stay out of it. Come on—let's go bake some cookies."

"I'll be there in a minute," Chloe said.

As soon as her dad was in the kitchen, Chloe made her way to Sandy's room. She tapped softly on the door, and then knocked again, louder, until she heard Sandy's voice.

"Come in."

Once again, Chloe found Sandy curled up on the bed, with Elsa in her arms. But this time, Chloe got right to the point. "What's wrong?" she asked.

"My dad called," Sandy said. "He was so excited. He said that the roads should be clear enough that he could get here tomorrow in time for dinner."

"Seriously?" Chloe squealed. "That's awesome!"

"Yeah—I mean, it would've been," Sandy replied. "But my mom said no! I hate her so much!"

133

"Wait—why?" Chloe asked. "This fixes everything! You'll get to see your dad on Christmas, and he doesn't have to spend the holiday all alone. It's perfect!"

"Tell it to my mom," Sandy said. "She wouldn't even discuss it! She said it would be awkward for everybody, and really unfair to you and your dad."

"Unfair? To us?" Chloe asked. "I don't get it."

"Don't ask me to spell it out for you," Sandy said, rolling over to face the wall. "Ask my mom."

Chloe sat there for another moment, trying to think of something to say, before she finally realized that there was nothing she *could* say. *Dad was right,* she thought. *We need to stay out of this.*

So without another word, Chloe slipped out of Sandy's room. She didn't feel like making cookies anymore, either. She'd rather sit with Charlie and take care of him.

❄ ❄ ❄

Charlie didn't get sick again that afternoon, but Chloe could tell he just wasn't feeling right. She decided that she wouldn't leave his side—not for anything.

Not even for a fancy Christmas Eve dinner at the lodge.

"I know the fireside is especially cozy," Dad said as the sun started to set. "But it's about time to get ready for dinner."

"I'm sorry, Dad," Chloe said. "I just can't leave Charlie. What if he gets worse, and I'm not here to take care of him? I could never forgive myself."

"I know how much you love Charlie, sweetie, but you've still got to eat dinner," Dad told her.

Chloe shrugged. "I'll just eat something here. Or you can bring me something back from the lodge. You should go ahead and have dinner up there! Jessica made a reservation, right?"

"Come on, you know I'm not going to leave you alone on Christmas Eve," Dad said gently. "Not even for dinner at the lodge. We'll find something in the kitchen and take care of Charlie together."

"We can all stay home tonight," Jessica added as she approached. "To be honest, I'm not really in the mood to get all dressed up again and trudge through the snow. I'd rather stay warm and cozy inside—all of us together."

Chloe flashed her a grateful smile. Now she wouldn't have to feel guilty for ruining Christmas Eve dinner.

"You know what?" Jessica continued. "We could have breakfast for dinner! There's bacon in the freezer and plenty of eggs in the fridge....I could make pancakes, or scrambled eggs, or—or both!"

"And don't forget the buttered toast," Dad joked. "If we were snowed in for another week we wouldn't be able to eat all that butter!"

❄ ❄ ❄

After dinner, Chloe took Charlie out again. To her relief, he seemed better. Standing outside Mistletoe Cottage, Chloe could see the little Christmas tree shining brightly through the windows. The cabin looked so warm and inviting on this frosty night.

Just then, Chloe heard footsteps crunching through the snow. The sound made her jump.

"Sorry to startle you," Jessica called out. "I had to get something from my car."

"Can I help?" Chloe asked.

"Maybe," Jessica said playfully. "If you promise not to peek!"

"That sounds mysterious," Chloe said with a laugh.

"It's just a few small presents I picked up in town yesterday," Jessica explained. "And I bought some wrapping supplies, too."

Chloe remembered the plain bag that contained Sandy's presents. It would look a lot better with some real trimming. "Do you have any extra ribbon I could use?" she asked.

"Sure," Jessica said. "Help yourself!"

Back in the cabin, Chloe rummaged around in the bag until she found a spool of red curling ribbon. "Thanks, Jessica," she said.

"My pleasure," she replied. Then Jessica turned to the others. "I have just a little bit of last-minute wrapping to do," she announced. "I'll be in my room—so *do not disturb*, unless you want your Christmas surprises to be ruined!"

Chloe slipped the ribbon in her back pocket. Sandy was holed up in the bedroom again, but Chloe was sure she could find a time to add the ribbon to Sandy's gift before Christmas morning. Maybe she could do it when Sandy brushed her teeth before bed.

The clock on the mantel began to chime; it was already nine o'clock. "What do you think—teatime?" Dad asked.

"Definitely," replied Chloe.

"You put the water on; I'll set the tray," Dad said. Chloe wondered what sort of Christmas Eve tea surprise he'd been able to manage through the snowstorm.

Just as the kettle started to sing, Sandy appeared. "I'm just getting a glass of water," she said awkwardly as she moved toward the sink.

"Oh," Dad said, sounding surprised. "I thought you'd be joining us for tea." He gestured to the tray, and that's when Chloe saw that he'd set it with three teacups—so smoothly that no one would've known that he had added one at the last minute for Sandy.

"Well…I don't want to, like, intrude," Sandy said.

"Not at all," Dad told her.

"Yeah! We have tea every night," Chloe said. "And on Christmas Eve, it's the last thing we do before going to bed."

"Room for one more?" Jessica asked as she appeared in the doorway.

Dad smiled at her—a special kind of smile that Chloe had never seen before. "Always," he replied, adding another cup.

He carried the heavy tea tray and set it on the table. Then Dad poured tea for everyone—first Jessica, then Sandy, and finally Chloe. She always took her tea the exact same way—a splash of cream and two small spoonfuls of sugar.

"Whoops," she said. "We forgot the sugar!"

Dad's eyes twinkled as he reached into his shirt pocket. "That's the Christmas Eve tea surprise!" he announced. "I bought these when we were shopping yesterday.... Of course, I thought we'd be having them back home, not in Mistletoe Cottage. Now, close your eyes and hold out your hand!"

Chloe immediately obliged. Her dad was such

a goofball about surprises, but his excitement was contagious. The paper bag rustled as Dad shook it—something light and delicate fell into her palm—

"Sugar snowflakes!" Chloe gasped. The tiny white snowflakes glittered with sugar crystals; they were almost too beautiful to dissolve in her tea. Chloe placed one on her tongue and tasted pure sweetness as it melted.

"Pretty cool, aren't they?" Dad asked. "Cool—get it? Because they're snowflakes?"

"Ha-ha, Dad, super funny," Chloe replied.

"They're beautiful," Jessica said, holding one up to the light.

"Look! It's a blizzard in my teacup!" Chloe announced as she poured the snowflakes into her tea.

"Too bad the real blizzard doesn't melt that fast," Sandy spoke up.

Chloe glanced over at her. It seemed like Sandy was trying to make a joke, but after all her tantrums, it fell flat—especially with Jessica.

"That's enough," Jessica said to her daughter. Then she turned back to Chloe and Dad. "How did you start having tea on Christmas Eve?"

"Dad and I have tea almost every night," Chloe explained. "Then, one year, on Christmas Eve, Dad had a surprise for our evening tea—Russian tea cakes! I was so excited about the special treat that on Christmas Eve the next year, he had scones and a special blackcurrant jam that came all the way from England and, oh, this was the best part—Christmas crackers, too!"

"Crackers?" Sandy asked. "Like saltines?"

Chloe laughed. "No, no, they're like these bright tubes with strings on the end, and when you pull them, they go *pop!* And all this cool stuff comes out. Paper crowns and confetti and little slips of paper with riddles and stuff."

Sandy tried to smile, but she couldn't quite manage it. She returned her teacup to the tray.

Too late, Chloe realized her mistake. Here she was, going on and on about special traditions with her dad—when Sandy would've given anything to see her own dad for Christmas. "I'm sorry!" Chloe told her. "I shouldn't have—"

"Why are you apologizing?" Jessica asked. "Did I miss something?"

"It's—" Chloe began.

"It's nothing," Sandy said, speaking right over her. "I'm just really tired. I think I'll go to bed."

That's just great, Chloe thought miserably. *I've upset Sandy so much that she'd rather go to bed than stay in the same room with me.*

Chloe had a feeling that Sandy wanted the same privacy she'd longed for earlier. But that was not easy to get in Mistletoe Cottage. *I've got to give Sandy some space tonight*, Chloe thought.

She stood up abruptly.

"Sandy—hang on," she said. "I'm going to get my pj's. I'll sleep on the couch tonight."

"You don't have to do that," Sandy mumbled.

"No, I want to," Chloe insisted. "That way I can keep an eye on Charlie—you know, to make sure he doesn't get worse overnight."

Jessica looked from Sandy to Chloe, then back to Sandy again. "Nobody's sleeping on the couch," she said firmly. "Let's keep Elsa in the kitchen so we can clean up her hair easily, and then Charlie can sleep in the bedroom."

"Mom! No!" Sandy argued. "Elsa sleeps with me every night! Why should she have to sleep all alone on Christmas Eve?"

Oh, great, Chloe thought. *Now Sandy's going to be even more upset with me.*

"Elsa will be fine," Jessica said. "She's a tough cat. Besides, if she wasn't constantly fighting with Charlie, they could both spend the night in the bedroom."

"But—but—what about Tom's allergies?" Sandy said.

"I think he'll be okay, since Elsa will just be in one spot," Jessica said, glancing over at Chloe's dad. Chloe could tell how much her dad wanted to stay out of it.

"I see. So in the morning, we'll just lock Elsa up again," Sandy snapped. "That's a great way to treat her, Mom. Really awesome."

"Can you even stop yourself?" Jessica asked. "It is *Christmas Eve.*"

"I know," Sandy shot back. "I know exactly what day it is."

Then she turned around and marched back to the bedroom.

At first, no one said anything. Then Chloe spoke up. "I really don't mind sleeping on the couch," she said as she pulled Charlie into her lap. "Neither one of us does."

Jessica shook her head. "You deserve to sleep in a bed," she said. "Sandy will cool down. She always does."

Just then, they heard Sandy stomping down the hall, carrying Elsa's food bowl. "Sorry to disturb you again. I didn't want Elsa to starve while she's all alone tonight."

Then Sandy caught a glimpse of Charlie on Chloe's lap, and her face softened. "How's Charlie? Is he okay?" she asked.

"I'm not sure," Chloe said honestly. "I think—I think he doesn't feel very good. But he hasn't gotten worse. Hopefully he'll be back to normal by morning."

"I hope so, too," Sandy replied.

By the time Chloe finished getting ready for bed and said good night to Dad and Jessica, Sandy was already in bed with the lights out. Chloe got into her bed as quietly as she could, grateful to feel the warmth of Charlie's body against her feet.

Scratch. Scratch. Scratch-scratch.

The sound of Elsa, scratching at the closed bedroom door, was unmistakable. And it made Chloe feel even worse about everything. *But Charlie needs me*, Chloe reminded herself. Staying close to him all night was the right thing to do.

Lying in bed, Chloe noticed for the first time that the bedroom had a skylight. The night sky was cloud-free, making it possible for Chloe to see an especially bright star twinkling through the darkness.

"Sandy?" Chloe whispered into the darkness. "Do you have a Christmas wish?"

There was no answer.

Maybe she's asleep, Chloe thought. *Or maybe she's just ignoring me.*

"I bet you wish you'd never have to see me or my dad again," Chloe answered her own question.

Across the room, Sandy stirred and sat up in bed. "That's not my Christmas wish," she replied. "I didn't answer because I'm not sure what my Christmas wish is."

Chloe was quiet as she waited for Sandy to continue.

"My wish used to be that my parents would get back together," Sandy finally said. "I'd wish that for everything: Christmas, birthdays, shooting stars, dandelions. But now...now I think I just wasted a lot of wishes. They're not going to get back together. Not ever. So I guess my Christmas wish is that I could see my dad tomorrow. But I know that's not going to happen, either."

Now Chloe really didn't know what to say. And Sandy seemed to understand that.

"Anyway, what's your Christmas wish?" Sandy asked.

Chloe stared up at that twinkling star and said what was in her heart: "All I want is for Charlie to be okay for Christmas," she replied.

"Yeah," Sandy said. "I want that, too."

Then Sandy flopped back into bed and rolled over to face the wall. Within a few minutes, she was asleep; Chloe could tell by her deep, even breathing. Chloe wished she could fall asleep, too. Instead, she tossed and turned, even after the rest of Mistletoe Cottage was quiet. Even after Elsa had stopped scratching at the door.

Suddenly, Chloe gasped and sat up in bed. Elsa—out in the living room—all by herself—with the presents! Presents that were wrapped with ribbon! Ribbon that could make Elsa seriously sick if she ate it!

In an instant, Chloe scrambled out of bed and raced into the living room. The tree was still lit, glowing softly in the dark room. Elsa, asleep by the still-warm fireplace, opened one eye, looked up at Chloe, and then went back to sleep.

Chloe examined each present carefully. To her relief, the ribbons and bows seemed intact. The edges were cleanly cut, and there weren't any teeth marks, either. There was no sign that Elsa had chewed on them.

Chloe breathed a sigh of relief. *That was a close call*, she thought. And she was determined to make sure that it wouldn't happen again. *Now I've got to find somewhere to hide these presents—a place where Elsa can't find them.*

But where?

Chloe stood back and scanned the room. There were no high-up shelves, and even if there were, there was no way to prevent Elsa from jumping to get them. *At least that's a problem we never had with Charlie*, she thought. His legs were too short to jump up high.

Chloe moved the presents to the kitchen counter, but it didn't seem safe enough. Elsa could easily jump up there and chew the ribbon. There was only one thing to do: Charlie and Elsa would have to switch places. That way, Elsa could sleep with Sandy, behind the closed door, while Chloe and Charlie camped out in the living room. It wasn't ideal, but Chloe knew she wouldn't sleep a wink if she was worrying about Elsa eating ribbons the whole time.

Chloe stroked Elsa's silky fur and could feel her purring. *She really is a sweet cat—when there aren't any dogs around*, Chloe thought. Then she carried Elsa back to the bedroom. In one fast motion, she dropped Elsa on Sandy's bed, then scooped up Charlie and scurried out of the room before Sandy awoke.

Back in the living room, Chloe curled up on the couch with the quilt pulled up to her chin. Charlie was already asleep by her feet. The last thing she heard was the clock on the mantel chiming midnight.

Christmas Day was here at last!

Chapter 12

Chloe's eyes popped open. It was still early—*very early*—the gray light that filtered through the windows told her that the sun wasn't even fully up yet. What had awakened her?

Then she heard it: Charlie's frantic whining at the door.

Oh no, Chloe thought. She knew what that meant. And it wasn't good.

She flung back the quilt and hurried over to the door. She'd have to go out in her pajamas—she didn't want to risk waking Sandy, and from the sound of Charlie's whining, there wasn't time to get dressed anyway—but hopefully she could put on her boots, at least—

"Hang on, Charlie," Chloe said as she jammed her feet into her boots. "I'm almost—"

His whining grew even louder and more urgent.

Chloe forgot all about her coat. She clipped the leash to Charlie's collar and flung open the door.

Poor Charlie couldn't even make it to the yard. He was sick right there, all over the doorstep.

"There, there," Chloe said, shivering in the cold—and powerless to help her pup feel better. "I'm so sorry, Charlie. I'm so sorry you're sick."

When Charlie was done, Chloe held him close and kissed the top of his head. Now there was no denying it: Something was seriously wrong with Charlie. Chloe was terrified. She didn't know if Charlie was going to be sick again, but it was too cold for them to stay outside any longer—especially since Chloe had left her coat in the cottage. She was wide awake, at least; the next time Charlie had to go out, she'd be ready to take him. They slipped back inside the cabin and heard—

"Merry Christmas!"

151

Chloe took one look at Dad and Jessica—and even Sandy, rubbing her sleepy eyes—and burst into tears.

"Chloe!" Dad exclaimed as he hurried over to her. "What's the matter?"

"It's—Charlie—" Chloe managed through her sobs. "He just got sick again. Really bad. Dad, I'm so worried! What if—"

Chloe's voice trailed off unexpectedly. She couldn't even bear to say the words.

"Hey, hey, let's not go there," Dad said soothingly as he wrapped his arms around Chloe. Then he pulled his phone out of his pocket. "I am going to send a message to Dr. Garcia, though."

Jessica glanced at the clock. "Are you sure? It's still pretty early," she said.

"Don't worry," Dad assured her. "Dr. Garcia has little kids. I'm sure she's been up for hours." Then he turned to Chloe. "Remember, Charlie's been sick like this before—and Dr. Garcia took excellent care of him."

"I know," Chloe whispered. "But don't you remember what Dr. Garcia said? If Charlie got sick even on his special diet…and I've been watching him really close, Dad! He hasn't had anything unusual to eat!"

"Ribbons!" Sandy suddenly exclaimed.

Everyone turned to look at her.

"Do you think he ate some ribbons, like Elsa did a few years ago?" Sandy continued. "If he did, he might need surgery, but then he'd be okay again after he recovered."

Chloe shook her head. "I don't think it was ribbons," she replied. "Charlie loves real food…he doesn't eat other stuff. Besides, I was so worried about the ribbons on the presents that I put them on the kitchen counter last night, right before I moved Elsa back into the bedroom. Charlie definitely couldn't reach them."

Sandy looked surprised. "That was you? I was wondering what happened when I woke up and found her asleep on my pillow."

"I was worried Elsa would get into the ribbons on the presents while we were all asleep," Chloe explained. "It seemed like the safest thing would be to keep Elsa out of the living room. So Charlie and I slept on the couch after all."

"I can't believe you'd do that for us," Sandy said. "I mean, your poor dog is really sick, and you were still looking out for Elsa?"

Chloe shrugged. "I'd hate for anything bad to happen to her...especially on Christmas," she replied.

Sandy impulsively reached out and gave Chloe a hug. "We're going to figure out what's wrong with Charlie," she told her. "We'll solve this mystery, no matter what it takes."

Dad's phone beeped then. "It's Dr. Garcia," he reported as his eyes scanned the screen. "She says it's really, really important for us to figure out if Charlie ate *anything* out of the ordinary. If he did, she thinks he will be okay. If not, and he gets sick again, we need to take him to the vet as soon as possible."

Chloe looked out the window at the heavy snow and wanted to cry again.

"Presents!" Jessica said suddenly. "Let's open the Christmas presents."

Who cares about presents at a time like this? Chloe wondered—but when she looked at Jessica's face, full of concern, she realized that Jessica was trying to distract Chloe from her worries.

Chloe took a deep breath and nodded. "Okay," she said. "I'll get them."

She crossed the room and took the gifts down from the counter. Jessica had done most of the shopping; she gave Chloe and Sandy each a funky crocheted hat, a handmade journal, and a small box of gourmet chocolates.

Then, to Chloe's surprise, Sandy handed her a present. It was the dog collar she'd been admiring in Pet Palace—the one that read DON'T FEED THE BEAST.

"Sandy! When—how—" she asked.

"Are you surprised?" Sandy asked. "I thought you'd see through my totally obvious lie about forgetting my wallet."

"So *that's* why you wouldn't let me come back with you!" Chloe laughed. Then she handed a present over to Sandy. "This is for you."

Sandy untied the ribbon and pulled the first present out of the bag.

"Chloe! It looks just like Elsa!" Sandy cried as she held up the cat ornament for everyone to see.

"I know!" Chloe replied. "The minute I saw that ornament, I *had* to get it. The kitty is even curled up on a pillow—"

"Just like Elsa curls up on my pillow!" Sandy finished for her.

"And *that* is the number one reason why Elsa's not allowed to sleep in my room," Jessica joked. "Only the pillow is good enough for her!"

"Thank you so much, Chloe," Sandy said gratefully as she hung the cat ornament on the little tree. "It's my favorite ornament ever!"

Chloe beamed with pleasure. "There's one more present in there," she said. "Though it's not exactly for you, I guess."

Sandy peered into the bag and burst out laughing. "Catnip mice? My favorite!" she joked.

"Sorry that they don't have any tails," Chloe said. "They were made of ribbon, so I cut them off so Elsa couldn't eat them."

156

"Thanks, I really appreciate it," Sandy said. "You won't believe how crazy she gets with catnip mice. She's even—actually, I'll let you see for yourself. Do you mind if I bring Elsa out for a minute?"

"Sure. I'll put Charlie back on his leash," Chloe said. She glanced around but didn't see her dog anywhere. "Charlie?" she called. Then Chloe turned to Dad and Jessica. "Have you seen Charlie?"

"I thought he was hiding next to you," Dad replied.

"So did I!" Chloe exclaimed. "He couldn't have gotten out. The cabin's so small—"

"Don't worry, we'll find him," Jessica promised her. "He might be hiding under some furniture. Animals often like to hide when they don't feel well. It's an instinct they have."

But Charlie would never hide from me, Chloe thought—not unless he was really, really sick. That hard, painful lump in her throat came back as she dropped to her knees to peer under the couch.

"Uh, guys?" Sandy's voice wafted through the living room. She'd gone to check the bedroom. "Can you come here?"

There was something in her voice that made

157

Chloe feel even more worried. She jumped to her feet and ran toward the bedroom, with Dad and Jessica following right behind her.

"Is it Charlie?" Chloe asked Sandy urgently. "Is he okay?"

"He looks fine to me," Sandy said, trying—and failing—not to laugh. "See for yourself!"

Sandy pointed into the bedroom. Chloe peeked through the doorway—and saw Charlie and Elsa curled up together on Sandy's pillow, both sound asleep!

"Am I really seeing that?" Chloe asked in astonishment. "Or is this some kind of hallucination?"

"It's real," Sandy assured her. "Look at them— they're best friends! It's a Christmas miracle!"

Everyone laughed so loud that Charlie and Elsa startled. They looked over at the door, obviously annoyed at being awakened. Then they curled up and went back to sleep!

"BFFs for sure," Sandy said, grinning. "Now they'll be inseparable. They'll take naps together, they'll play together, they'll eat together—"

Sandy's sudden gasp made Chloe jump. "Whoa—what's wrong?" she asked.

"The kitchen!" Sandy cried. "Come with me!"

Chloe didn't have a clue what was going on, but she followed Sandy to the kitchen anyway. Sandy pointed to a bowl on the floor, tucked away in the corner. "Elsa's food!" she said. "I'm so sorry, Chloe, I didn't even think—"

A flash of understanding lit up Chloe's eyes. "You think Charlie's been eating Elsa's food?" she asked.

"It would make sense, wouldn't it?" Sandy asked. "He got sick on Saturday after he was here—and had access to her food. On Sunday, though, he was fine—and that's the day that he *wasn't* here and *couldn't* have eaten any cat food."

"Then—yesterday—sick again, after we moved into Mistletoe Cottage," Chloe said. Everything was starting to make sense now. "And then I bet he ate even more cat food overnight while I was sleeping!"

"The bowl's empty," Sandy said. "I filled it up right before bed and left it in the kitchen—"

"Because *Elsa* was supposed to sleep in the living room!" Chloe realized.

"I've been wondering why she was eating so much!" Sandy exclaimed.

Jessica looked embarrassed. "Actually, I filled up Elsa's bowl yesterday, too," she said.

"But, Mom—that's my job," Sandy said.

"I know," Jessica replied. "But you've been so upset, I thought that maybe you forgot. You never let it get empty like that."

"Charlie!" Chloe groaned. "Why have you been pigging out on cat food?"

"No wonder Elsa was chasing him all around the cabin," Dad said. "She was mad at him for eating all her food!"

As everyone laughed again, Dad sent a quick text to update Dr. Garcia. "I'm sure this was the problem," he said. "But we'll wait for Dr. Garcia's expert opinion."

Almost immediately after Dad sent the text, his phone beeped. A broad smile crossed his face as he read Dr. Garcia's response.

"Well? What did she say?" Chloe asked.

"Here," Dad said as he passed her the phone. "I think you should read it for yourself."

> Unlimited access to cat food could definitely cause Charlie's symptoms. I'm glad you figured it out! He should be back to normal once he's eating his own food again. Remind Charlie that he should avoid overindulging—even at the holidays. Merry Christmas!

When Chloe read Dr. Garcia's text aloud, everyone cheered—and as she looked from Dad to Jessica to Sandy, she could see that they were all as happy and relieved as she was. Chloe was so happy that her smile stretched across her face. Charlie was going to be okay. Her Christmas wish had come true!

Chapter 13

Later that day, Chloe and Sandy bundled up and went outside to play in the snow. The sun was shining much brighter, and Chloe had a funny feeling that the roads would be cleared even sooner than they expected.

"Let's build something out of snow," Chloe suggested.

"Sure," Sandy said. "A snowman?"

"Maybe," Chloe said. "Or we could build a snow-castle. You know, like a sandcastle, but made of snow."

"That sounds cool," Sandy said. "Oh! What if we built Santa's village? With little cabins for the elves?"

"And a barn for the reindeer!" Chloe exclaimed. "And we can decorate everything with pebbles and pine needles—"

"And bits of ribbon," Sandy said, laughing. "Since Elsa is strictly an indoor cat."

"Love it," Chloe said. "I might even try to build Santa's sleigh."

The girls were quiet as they went to work, packing snow into the shape of tiny houses and roads. After a while, Chloe started speaking.

"You made my Christmas wish come true," she said, staring at the snow in her hands. "Charlie's going to be okay, and it's all because you figured out what was wrong with him. I don't know how to thank you, Sandy. I'll never be able to thank you enough."

"Thank *me*?" Sandy asked in surprise. "You don't have to thank me for anything. I've been..."

Sandy's voice trailed off, but Chloe stayed focused on the snow she was sculpting. She didn't look at her...and she didn't say a word.

"Let's just say I'm not proud of myself," Sandy said. "I wish I could start the trip over again and do everything differently. I'm sorry I was so mean. And I'm sorry I ruined the trip."

"You definitely didn't ruin it!" Chloe said right away. "You figured out what was wrong with Charlie.... You bought him an awesome new collar.... We had so much fun shopping and snow tubing and taking selfies at the party.... I mean, I did...."

Chloe glanced up just in time to see Sandy smiling at her.

"I did, too," Sandy said. "Anyway, I just wanted to tell you...next time, it will be even better."

"Next time?" Chloe asked. "Do you know something I don't know?"

Sandy shrugged. "I just figured we'd all take another trip sometime. My mom is obviously crazy about your dad."

"And he feels the same way about her," Chloe said. "Obviously. So when do you think our next trip will be?"

"Well..." Sandy began. "Presidents' Day weekend is coming up. I wish it could be sooner, though."

"What about Martin Luther King Day? That's next month," Chloe suggested.

"Or how about New Year's?" Sandy joked. "That's, like, next week!"

As the girls laughed, they heard the sound of a pickup truck driving over the gravel back roads. Chloe realized it was the first vehicle she'd heard since the storm hit. "I wonder who that is," she said. "Maintenance crew, maybe?"

"Maybe," Sandy said. "Too bad they have to work on Christmas."

The girls went back to building their snow village.

"You know," Chloe said, "the roads must be better if a truck…"

Just then, the truck appeared. It was as bright and shiny as Rudolph's nose. And it was driving toward Mistletoe Cottage.

Sandy stood up abruptly as the truck parked on the side of the road.

"Do you—" Chloe began.

"Dad!" Sandy screamed joyfully. "Dad! Dad! You're here!"

A tall, bearded man stepped out of the truck. His smile was identical to Sandy's as she ran through the snow and catapulted into his arms.

"Merry Christmas, baby girl!" he said as he squeezed Sandy in a bear hug.

The sight of Sandy and her dad, reunited for Christmas, made Chloe want to cry happy tears.

"Chloe!" Sandy exclaimed. "Come meet my dad!"

"Hi, I'm Jason," Sandy's dad said.

"Chloe is Tom's daughter," Sandy explained. Then her smile fell.

"What's wrong, Sandy-Crab?" Jason asked. Chloe tried not to giggle at the nickname, which—sometimes—suited Sandy perfectly.

"I'm—Dad—Mom said you shouldn't come," Sandy said awkwardly. "I'm sorry—I don't—"

"Don't give it another thought," Jason told her. "Your mom and I talked last night, and I talked to Tom, too. They invited me for Christmas dinner if the roads were clear enough to drive."

"They did?" Sandy exclaimed.

Jason nodded. "But I told them not to tell you—just in case I couldn't make it through," he said. "I didn't want to disappoint you. Not on Christmas."

"You could never disappoint me," Sandy told her dad. "I'm sorry, though…we already opened presents."

Jason kissed the top of her head. "That's okay—I didn't bring any, since I didn't have some for everybody. That doesn't mean I came empty-handed, though. You girls want to help me carry in these groceries? I've brought everything we need for a Christmas feast!"

"Thank goodness!" Chloe exclaimed. "Otherwise I think we were going to be stuck eating butter."

"It's a long story," Sandy said when she saw her dad's confused look. "Let's go inside and meet Tom. I think you'll like him.... He's really nice...."

Chloe grabbed a grocery bag and trailed behind Sandy and Jason. As she watched them laughing together, she realized that now Sandy's Christmas wish had come true, too. *The bright star we saw last night must have had extra Christmas magic*, Chloe thought.

A smile spread across Chloe's face as she remembered what her dad had said about how his family had changed, in ways he had never expected: not ruined, not broken, but different. Bigger.

And impossible to imagine any other way!

Not finished celebrating the season yet? Check out these other feel-good books in the series: